The
Enemy
Within
A Dystopian Novel

Graham Watkins

ISBN-13: 9781093338539

Matt's piercing screams could be heard two blocks away. The terror he'd planned to create had gone wrong ... horribly, agonisingly wrong. And now the skinny youth with the scruffy tangle of red hair was ablaze... burning to death in a London street near the mosque he'd wanted to destroy.

Matthew Blake, lonely and gullible, is a victim of hatred, racism and fear. Just one of many.

CONTENTS

ACKNOWLEDGMENTS

To those people who have encouraged the writing of this novel and gently corrected my mistakes, of which there have been too many to count..

CHAPTER 1

Acrid smoke filled the air - vile tasting - stomach churning. The youth lit the wick and raised the petrol bomb ready to throw it. Tear gas stung his eyes. A line of black body armour and shields moved menacingly forward. A police cameraman filmed. The youth stepped from behind the overturned car, choked and stumbled. Petrol and oil ran down his sleeve and ignited. He dropped the bottle. It shattered, engulfing him in flames; a screaming, flailing, human torch. Rioters scattered. The police line advanced, batons banging shields with every step, the sound echoing across the street. They separated, passing beyond the burning youth, onwards, towards the retreating mob. They broke ranks and charged, clearing protestors from the East London Mosque, shouting, herding the crowd into alleyways and side streets. People cowered in doorways, behind cars, railings - anywhere to escape the brutal onslaught. A woman fell. She screamed and was carried away to an ambulance.

Then, it was over. Whitechapel Road was still, a confusion of broken banners 'Britain First' 'Rule Britannia' 'Taking our country back' 'Defend blasphemy' 'Allah is Gay' - meaningless words, trampled underfoot. Shattered glass and a woman's shoe lay on the pavement. The youth, silent now, fell, a lifeless form, his smouldering arm raised in ghoulish defiance. A green helmeted paramedic bent down to examine him and retched, overwhelmed by the smell of burnt flesh. He shook his head. A fireman sprayed the blackened corpse with foam then watched, bemused, as a cleric stepped purposefully through the shattered doors of the prayer hall and began to sweep away broken glass. The cleric stopped, picked up the woman's shoe, looked at it momentarily and dropped it in a litter bin.

Simon Reece was working from home. The thirty nine year old businessman had important documents to study. He gathered up papers strewn across the coffee table, arranged them neatly beside a laptop and went out onto the balcony. Voices and laughter floated up from boaters on the River Cam. Beyond the river, the spires of Trinity College stood majestic against the skyline. Cambridge had been good to Simon. He'd read computer science at Trinity. Completing his Master's Degree he'd stayed and started Harland Digital in a small room above Mr. Johal's shop on Russell Street. The business thrived and grew to occupy modern offices in Cambridge Science Park. Simon thought back to the day he signed the lease for the new offices; a proud day. Harland and the eighty people he employed were everything to Simon but all things must end and that was why he was hurting.

Simon wasn't married. Sure, he was good looking, he'd had girlfriends but they never lasted. His love was the business. He neglected them and they soon moved on except, that is, one. Julie was different. She'd clung on, possessive and demanding until he came home late once too often. She swore at him, calling him a selfish bastard and worse. They fought. He lost his temper and told her to pack - to get out.

Simon returned to the documents on the table. He made notes in the margins; questions to ask his lawyer.

2

The contract to sell Harland, written by the American buyers, was complex. He had to understand it. Too much was at stake. He stopped for a break and turned on the television.

"The dead man has been named by police as Matthew Blake, nineteen, unemployed, from Muswell Hill," said the reporter. "He died from burns attempting to throw a petrol bomb. Blake was a known member of the white supremacist faction 'Britain First' banned earlier this year." Video of the riot appeared on the screen. "Other anti Muslim demonstrations have taken place in Birmingham and Leeds. The Home Secretary has chaired a meeting of the Cobra Emergency Committee."

The phone rang. "Mr. Simon Reece? This is Sergeant Davies, Thames Valley Police."

"I'm afraid I have some bad news."

Simon muted the television.

"There's been an accident, a car crash, involving your parents. They're both dead. I'm very sorry, Sir."

Simon felt numb and sick as he drove to the hospital.

The mortuary was cold, clinical. Simon watched as a tray slid out of the refrigerator and his father's head was uncovered. "He looks asleep," he said and touched the cold skin with his hand. He saw his mother's face and turned away.

That night Simon drank to dull his senses but there was no escape from the pain, the anger and the emptiness.

He woke early washed pain killers down with coffee, phoned an undertaker and made arrangements for the funerals.

Reverend Griffiths looked around and smiled reassuringly. Villagers filled the cemetery, crowding around the open grave. Others, standing in the lane, peered over churchyard wall.

"Eternal rest grant unto them, O Lord," intoned the vicar, his voice crisp and loud.

"And let perpetual light shine upon them," mumbled the mourners.

"May they rest in peace."

"Amen."

"May their souls and the souls of the faithful departed, through the mercy of God, rest in peace," said the vicar. He closed his prayer book, made the sign of the cross and stepped back. The air was damp and still. The mourners stood silent, awkward. Simon Reece looked down at the open grave, at the two coffins stacked, one above the other. He picked up a handful of earth and threw it. The damp earth landed with a thud on his mother's coffin. A light drizzle began to fall. Mourners started to drift away.

"The ladies have arranged refreshments at the house," announced the vicar. He unfurled an umbrella and turned to Simon, "I'll walk back with you."

"You go on. I want a few moments with Mum and Dad."

The vicar offered the umbrella but Simon waved him away. The vicar shrugged and left, walking with others back to the dead couple's house.

Simon was alone in the graveyard. The rain was heavier now, drumming rhythmically on the coffins. Simon turned up the collar of his jacket. Drops of icy water ran down his neck. He watched the earth he'd tossed on his mother's coffin turn to mud and trickle away.

"On top again Mum," muttered Simon. "You always did have the last word." He remembered how his father would retreat to the shed, lost for words, when she'd made her point. Simon wiped water from his face and shuddered.

"Goodbye Mum, Dad." He turned and hurried from the graveyard.

Mrs Williams was pouring teas in the kitchen. Other women were distributing sandwiches, and fussing as village women do at funerals.

"There you are," said Mrs Williams as Simon came through the door, "Would you like some tea?"

Simon took his jacket off, hung it on the back of a chair and dried his hair with a towel. He took a cup to the sitting room and stood in the doorway listening to the conversation.

"Jack loved his garden and tinkering in his shed," said a neighbour. "He would be outside in all weathers, even on days like this," he pointed to the window.

"Do you remember when he won first prize in the show with that enormous onion?" asked another. "When Sally made gallons of onion soup and filled the freezer with it. I bet, if you look Simon, there's still some there. He never did like onion soup."

Simon smiled and made a mental note to empty the freezer before he went home. The conversation continued with other anecdotes - as if the villagers wanted to enjoy the moment, to celebrate the lives of Simon's parents. The wake became sombre and they talked quietly about the car crash. Why had nothing been done about that awful piece of road? Two innocent lives wasted. It was a disgrace. By five o'clock the rain had stopped and the house was almost empty. People had made their excuses, offered their condolences to Simon and slipped away. Simon helped Mrs Williams clear the sitting room and wash the plates.

"What will you do now?" she asked, putting on her coat.

"I have to sort out Mum and Dad's affairs so I am going to stay here for a few days," he replied.

"Your parents were lovely people. Your dad was a gentleman. I never once heard him raise his voice or argue with anyone and your mum well..." Mrs Williams smiled. "I was very fond of them both. If you need anything, I'm only next door." She gave Simon a hug and left.

He picked up a glass, returned to the sitting room and emptied the last of the sherry from bottle in the sideboard. His father's slippers were still under the coffee table. They looked ridiculous, small and lost.

The next morning, Simon was up early. He shaved, showered and ate a bowl of cereal, stood in the kitchen. The television was on. He watched, uninterested as a political news story developed. An excited reporter described the stunning election success of Max Roberts becoming the leader of The National People's Party. The scene cut to Max Roberts waving triumphantly to his supporters then to a doorstep interview.

"Mr. Roberts. Why do you think your victory was so overwhelming?"

A microphone was pushed forward. "The National People's Party is ready to take our great country forward. People are sick and tired of weak leadership from this government. The NPP have elected me with a mandate to stand firm for our beliefs and protect our citizens from any threat. It's time to deal with the terrorists, the illegal immigrants and those foreigners who think they can use our National Health Service for free. It's time for the Prime Minister to resign, to step aside and let us deal with the poison that's in our country."

"If you become Prime Minister would you cut all ties with Europe?" shouted the reporter.

A minder pushed the microphone aside. Roberts and his entourage swept on, past the media scrum.

The bulletin cut back to the studio presenter. "Whatever your opinion is about right wing politics, it's clear Max Roberts is popular and the next general election will be a real fight."

Simon turned the television off. Just gone eight o'clock; the office would be open. Simon rang the number.

"How was the funeral?" asked his secretary.

"Wet and muddy. Joy, I'm going to need a couple of days off. Cancel my appointments and ask John Hume to meet the Americans when they fly in on Friday. Tell him to explain and offer my apologies. He's to show the guys from Systron Security around the offices and entertain them over the weekend. I'll be back on Monday. We can do the formal stuff then."

"There are some more questions from Systron's legal team. Arrived by email yesterday," said Joy, "Shall I pass them on to the lawyers?"

"That's what we pay them for."

"Simon, are you alright?.. Did everything go OK? I mean, yesterday?"

"I'm fine," he paused. "Thanks for asking. Is there anything else?"

"Nothing that we can't handle. We'll see you on Monday. Bye," said Joy.

Simon phoned an estate agent and a number offering a house clearance service then he started going through drawers and cupboards. He found copies of his parent's wills. Everything was left to him. They weren't rich. The house remortgaged to fund their retirement. Simon added up the money; three hundred and forty pounds in the bank, six pounds in Dad's wallet, two hundred and twenty-six pounds in his mother's purse. Simon put the cash in his pocket and phoned his lawyer.

"It's Simon Reece from Harland Digital calling. Neville Phillips please?"

"I'll see if he's available," replied the receptionist and connected the call.

"Neville, it's Simon. You won't have heard but my parents were killed in a car crash. They were buried yesterday."

"I'm sorry to hear that Simon. Are you at the office?"

"No. I'm at Mum and Dad's house. I need you to take care of the probate."

"I would except I'm a corporate lawyer... Don't worry. One of the partners will deal with it. Do you have any paperwork?"

"Thanks. I'll drop off the wills and anything else I find when I get back on Monday. One other thing. There's going to be an inquest. Is there anything I need to do for it?"

"I see." The lawyer paused. "Probably not but, as next of kin, you might be asked for a statement about their health, mental state, that sort of thing. Best to wait and see if the coroner's office asks for one. Have you spoken to Joy? She's just emailed me more questions from the Americans. They really are being super cautious. Asking for more information about Harland Digital's patent rights."

"She told me," said Simon, "It's posturing. A tactic to introduce uncertainty, to lower the price at the last minute. I've got to go. There's a lot of sorting out to be done here."

Simon collected together a few items; his father's cufflinks, the gold watch he was given when he retired and his mother's jewellery. He picked up a plaster dog he'd bought his mother on a school trip. Tat, he thought and threw it in the bin.

He opened his father's wardrobe - two pairs of trousers and a shabby tweed jacket with leather cuffs. Dad never wanted new clothes. Waste of money, he would say. His mother's wardrobe was twice as large. Simon pushed his arm between the hangers and pulled out a flowery dress. The price tag was still attached.

A battered brown suitcase was sitting on top of the wardrobe. It was heavier than he expected. As he lifted it down the handle came off and the case landed with a thump on the bed. He pulled at the lid - locked.

The doorbell rang. A van with 'Dan the Clearance Man' painted in crude red letters on the side was parked outside the house. A shabbily dressed man was at the front door a second standing by the van.

"That was quick. I wasn't expecting you until this afternoon."

"I'm Dan. You said you wanted the house emptied right away. This is my boy Jack," said the older man and offered a tattooed hand.

"Where do you want to start?"

"We'll have a look around and I'll make you an offer," said Dan and went into the sitting room. His son followed.

"This one's for the tip," said Dan, pointing at the settee.

'Why? What's wrong with it?" asked Simon.

"No fire label. Can't sell it." He glanced at the sideboard and grunted. "Brown furniture, nobody wants it these days."

Simon followed the men upstairs.

They stripped a bed. Dan pointed to a stain. "Mattress's been pissed on," They moved to the next room.

"This one's OK. Chest of drawers is tidy."

Jack opened the wardrobes. "Rags."

"Yeah. Charity shop," said his dad.

"Some of the clothes are new," said Simon.

Dan shrugged. "Old people's clothes."

"There's some good china in the kitchen and dad's tools are in the shed."

"Tools?" asked Jack, "What sort of tools?"

"A motor mower, gardening tools that sort of thing," replied Simon, "And some woodworking tools, planes, chisels. I don't know if they're worth much."

Dan finished his inspection. "Two hundred quid and we'll take everything."

"Two hundred pounds. I was expecting more."

"Look, old people's houses are filled with crap nobody wants. Most of it ends up at the dump."

"I don't know... I'll think about it," said Simon.

"You won't get anymore. If it wasn't for the tools you'd be paying us to clear the house... "

Simon didn't answer.

"Alright... Two hundred and twenty we'll clear the house now. It's up to you."

"OK," said Simon and watched the men load the van. He was standing in the hall when Jack came down the stairs with the brown suitcase.

"Hang on," said Simon.

"Do you want it?" asked Jack.

Simon nodded. "I'd better go through it."

Five minutes later they were gone leaving Simon alone in the empty house. He wandered from room to room. The house felt bigger, sterile, no longer a home. Two hundred and twenty pounds, he still had the money in his hand, had cauterised any connection he had to his life there.

A BMW convertible, arrived and out stepped a well manicured woman, thirtyish, confident; a professional. "Beverley Manning from Parker and Smith, estate agents. Before I start Mr. Reece, I have to ring my office and let them know I'm here. It's company policy. For security." She held a mobile to her ear. "Give me half an hour to measure and make some notes and we'll have a chat... Hello. Yes I'm with Mr. Reece now."

"When you've finished," said Simon. "I'll be in the garden." He took the suitcase outside, sat on the patio wall and forced the lock. It was full of papers. An envelope on the top contained his University Degree, another school reports. A press cutting carefully placed in a clear plastic wallet told of when he broke his arm playing rugby. Turning it over he saw a photograph of himself proudly holding his plaster cast.

Simon read the faded newsprint and thought of his mother. The suitcase would have been hers. Photographs spilled from plastic bags, of Simon on the beach, blowing out birthday candles and playing in the garden. He pulled out childish drawings that were once stuck to the fridge. He shut the case and sat in the sunshine. Things were moving more quickly than he'd imagined. If Beverley Manning did her job he could drive home tonight. Simon went to the shed and ran his hand along the workbench he'd helped his father build.

"Mr. Reece?"

Simon emerged and shut the door. "Please, call me Simon."

"I need to take some pictures of the house from the garden."

"How much is it worth?" asked Simon.

"The market is slow at the moment. If you want to sell quickly, I suggest we ask two hundred and twenty thousand pounds." She smiled. "What do you think?"

"That's fine," said Simon. "I'll need you to handle the viewings. I won't be here. What do you charge?"

"If we're exclusive, one and a half percent." She smiled again.

"Do you think it'll sell quickly?"

"At that price there's no reason why not. I sell houses and I'd like to sell yours."

"Good. I'll give you a set of keys."

"That's fantastic," said Beverley. "Let me have your email address. I'll get draft particulars and a contract to you tomorrow. As soon as you send it back, I'll list the house and send the details out to potential buyers."

Simon handed the keys to the estate agent and returned to Cambridge. That evening he poured a large whisky and sat on the settee with the suitcase at his feet. A Mozart clarinet concerto played quietly in the background.

Removing the contents of the case his thoughts wandered back to happier times. Here, lovingly saved by his mother, was his childhood, documented and stored for posterity. It was because of her Simon had gone to Trinity College.

"You'll never amount to anything unless you push yourself," she'd declared. "Your father's a good man and I love him but he's afraid of failure. Never pushed himself. Don't end up like him."

Simon pulled a large brown envelope from the bottom of the case. It was addressed to his parents and looked official. He read the postmark '1981'. Simon would have been three.

The envelope split as he removed the contents. A birth certificate caught his eye. 'Certified copy of entry'. He continued reading, 'Name of child - Simon Jackson, sex of child - male, name, address and occupation of adopters.' That's odd. He stopped reading. It wasn't a birth certificate.

The adopters, Jack William Reece and Sally Elizabeth Reece, were his parents. What did it mean? Who was Simon Jackson and why was he adopted? Simon got up, poured himself another drink and spread the documents across the dining table. The adoption certificate was registered in the General Register Office at Bristol. He picked up another document, a 'Change of Name Deed,' changing Simon Jackson's family name to Reece. A copy of a hand written letter, consented to the change of name was attached, signed by both of his parents.

CHAPTER 2

That night Simon couldn't sleep. His mind was racing. He relived the funeral in vivid detail. The mud on his mother's coffin - but she wasn't his mother. The deal he was trying to do, the biggest in his life, came crowding in. The Americans were coming. He was adopted. The urine stained mattress. Beverley Manning, slick and attractive. Why hadn't they told him? Who were his real parents? Were they alive? Why had they given him away?

At five o'clock he got up, showered and drove to the office. The car radio was on.

"...Four men, believed to be terrorists used a van to mow down pedestrians in a London street. When it crashed they abandoned it and attacked everyone they met. Dozens were stabbed," said the reporter. "Two attackers were shot dead. The others are being hunted by police. There are multiple deaths. Fleets of ambulances are ferrying the wounded to hospitals across London. The public are warned not to approach the men but to dial 999 immediately."

A sound bite, from the Prime Minister's press conference, followed. "This is a heinous, evil crime. Our hearts go out to the dead, the injured and their families but the British people will not be bowed. We will stand together and face the terrorists down. Their cowardly acts are despicable and unworthy of any religion. Now isn't the time to make new policies or overreact. Let the police and security services do their job and later, when we have all the facts, we will make the right political decisions. Lessons will be learned."

Simon stopped, posted an envelope containing his parent's wills through the solicitor's letterbox and got back into the car.

"Here's what Max Roberts leader of the National People's Party said just a few moments ago," said the radio presenter.

"This is the fourth terrorist attack this month. Of course we grieve for the dead and pray for the wounded but grieving and praying isn't enough. The Prime Minister talks about waiting for all the facts and learning lessons. I ask her, 'How many more deaths do there have to be before we have all the facts?' It's time to take action against the enemies who want to destroy us; to stop pussyfooting about. We are in a war and it is a war that, if elected, the NPP will win. We will be publishing our manifesto next week and it will include a list of effective counter measures designed to stop these criminals, to destroy them and their organisation. The NPP needs everyone's support. Vote for the National People's Party and I promise you we will stop the terrorists."

"So the NPP are taking a much harder line," said the presenter as Simon's car pulled into the car park.

"Someone needs to do something," muttered Simon and turned off the radio.

Simon had cleared a backlog of emails and was drinking coffee, when his personal assistant arrived.

Joy put her head through the office door. "I wasn't expecting you back until Monday."

"I had to come back but I'm taking the rest of today off," said Simon. "Did you tell John to collect the Americans and look after them?"

"He's going to the airport this afternoon," replied Joy. "I've booked them into Madingley Hall. John's arranged a tour of the colleges and he's borrowing a Darwin College punt to take them on the river on Saturday."

Simon smiled at the idea of three high flying American businessmen being punted along the River Cam. "Good idea. Tell John not to fall in and, Joy, book a table for Saturday evening at The Chop House. I'll join them for dinner."

Simon briefed the software team telling them what to show the Americans and went back to his office. He shut the door and made a personal call.

"Hello." It was a woman's voice.

"Julie, it's Simon." A child screeched in the background.

"What do you want?"

"I need to talk to you."

"You haven't needed me for five years, remember?" Her reply was icy.

"Please, I need your help," pleaded Simon.

"You need my help!"

"I've learned something important about myself and don't know who else to talk to."

"....What? What have you learned?"

"My parents are dead, killed in a car crash... You see, the thing is Julie, they weren't my real mum and dad."

"He hit me," squealed a voice.

"Just a minute... Right you two. Go in the other room NOW, and play quietly," Julie came back to the phone. "Meet me at Enzo's Coffee Shop at twelve." The voice was calm. "And Simon, we can talk but it's over between us." The line went dead.

On his way to the coffee shop, Simon bought a newspaper. 'Terrorist attack - threat level critical,' said the headline. Photographs of last night's atrocity filled the paper. He read a report about hate preacher Masood Khan's release. His appeal to the European Court of Human Rights had been upheld. The article quoted Max Roberts criticising the judgment saying it was crass and ill judged.

"Bloody ridiculous," muttered Simon. "Roberts is right. Khan should never have been released."

Julie arrived and sat down opposite him.

He folded the paper and fetched her a latte. "You look good. How are the children?"

"Fine thanks. They're at playschool. I collect them at one o'clock."

She looked directly at Simon. "How do you feel?"

"Confused."

"That's how I felt when I found out."

"I remember," said Simon. "Did you find her?"

"You remember, do you?... I needed you and you dumped me," she hissed. "You threw me out."

Simon looked down. "I'm sorry. There was a lot going on; the business."

"Yeah! the business."

They sat quietly, both looking at the table.

"Did you find her; your real mother?" Asked Simon.

"Yes."

"That's good."

Not really," said Julie quietly. "She refused to see me. When the adoption agency suggested a reunion she told them to get lost. All they told me was she's happily married with two children and three grandchildren. How's that for a kick in the tee...."

A hissing noise from behind the counter interrupted her as the espresso machine frothed hot milk.

Simon reached across the table to touch her hand.

She pulled away. "Are you going to try and find your real parents?"

"I need to know the truth about myself. Are they alive? Do I have any brothers or sisters? But where do I start?" He asked.

"Let it go, Simon. Get on with your life. Forget them, unless you want rejection and your heart broken." Julie looked up and held his gaze. "But you won't, will you?" She pushed her cup away and stood. "You might begin with the Adoption Contact Register. That's where I started. Don't ring me again."

Simon sat looking at her empty chair. Had he loved her? Probably not, otherwise why did he dump her when her life had become complicated, when she needed him most? The truth was, she had been an emotional mess, a tearful distraction - easy to eject from his life. Simon felt uncomfortable. He had been wrong to expect her to help, had no right to reopen old wounds. She'd found someone else and built a new life but the pain of rejection and insecurity was still there.

CHAPTER 3

Simon felt excited, almost jubilant as he started searching ancestry websites. He typed 'Simon Jackson son of Mr. and Mrs. Jackson,' 'Simon Reece adopted by Jack and Sally Reece'. Nothing... It was hopeless. With no starting point he was lost. He poured another drink and tried Facebook. It was useless. There were thousands of Jacksons.

What did Julie say? "Begin with the Adoption Contact Register." That was it. He found the 'Adoption Contact Register' website, downloaded an application form and started to fill it in. But what if his real parents were not on the register? What if they were but wanted nothing to do with him...

Shit! The application needed Simon's date and place of birth. What were they? He had no idea.

Simon searched the suitcase for a birth certificate. Surely his mother would have kept a copy. He emptied the envelopes unfolding every scrap of paper... Nothing. Without a date of birth he couldn't register. He was frustrated and tired. Where could he get a copy? The General Register Office... maybe they would have one. He completed an application, with the details he knew, pressed send and went to bed. It was a long shot but he had to try.

It was dark when the telephone rang.

"Simon, have you seen the news?" Joy's voice was shrill. "A bomb has gone off at the American Air Force base at Mardenheath. There are mass casualties."

Simon looked at the time. It was six o'clock. He got out of bed. "Ring John Hume. Tell him to meet me at Madingley Hall. We need to make sure the Americans don't panic and bolt. . . And, Joy, we need to keep them busy. Get the software team into work. I want the place to hum when we arrive with the Americans. We're going to do the site visit for Systron Security today."

Simon switched on the television. The BBC news channel was reporting the bomb attack. A reporter stood in front of the gates of the American base. The bomb had exploded in a crowded cinema on the base at five past midnight as American servicemen and their families were watching a football game being beamed from the US.

Simon listened to the radio as he drove to Madingley Hall. "...The Prime Minister will be chairing a Cobra emergency committee at eleven o'clock."

There was a siren. Simon pulled over. An ambulance screamed past.

"Twenty three dead and more than fifty, including children, wounded, many with life threatening injuries," said the radio presenter.

The United States President spoke next. "This is a wicked, evil attack on men, women and children. . . Little babies. We don't know who's responsible but we will find them, trust me. Our people are already working on it. I've ordered all military personnel to return to their bases which are now in lockdown. No one who is not security vetted by our own guys will be allowed to enter. American civilians are instructed to leave the UK immediately."

"Shit," said Simon and turned the radio off. He'd arrived at the American's hotel.

The Americans from Systron Security were in the restaurant having breakfast. Simon recognised the big Texan C.J. Hunt immediately.

"Simon! Good to see ya. Pull up a chair," called C.J. He waved Simon over. "Mam," he called to a waitress. "Can we get a coffee for our guest?" He grabbed Simon's hand and crushed it. "Guys, this is Simon Reece. He's the brains behind Harland Digital. Simon this is Ben Fripp, our lawyer and the scrawny one is Nico Synful. Nico's our software guy."

Simon looked at the attractive brunette next to C.J. "Nico?"

"Short for Nicola," she explained.

They shook hands and he sat down. The waitress arrived with a cup and a pot of coffee.

"A bombs gone off. What the hell's happening?" asked C.J.

"Mardenheath, where the big American cargo planes land," explained Simon. "It's a huge airbase, thousands of servicemen and their families. Apparently the bomb went off during a football game. . . "

"We heard on the news this morning. Dallas Cowboys were playing the L.A. Rams," interrupted Fripp.

"Hell. I saw the game in my room," said C.J. "Cowboys won. Nobody said anything about a bomb."

Fripp poured coffee. "Was it Muslim terrorists? Revenge for Guantanamo? And this guy Khan! If he's a terrorist why was he released? You Brits are too soft."

"They've not said who's responsible," replied Simon. "As for Khan, I agree. He should still be in prison."

"Your man Roberts has the right idea. Make him Prime Minister and the terrorists will get what they deserve," said Fripp and sipped his coffee. "He was on the TV this morning announcing some protocols to destroy the bad guys."

"Protocols? That's news to me. What were they?" asked

Simon.

The lawyer put down his cup. "It's an idea our President's peddling. A DNA database for everyone in the country, implanted identity chips like you have in dogs and. . ."

"Hell. That's a great idea," injected C.J. "Meanwhile, until you Brits sort this mess out we've been told to skedaddle home. Stupid if you ask me."

John Hume arrived and pulled up a chair.

"Listen C.J. There's no need to run away," said Simon. "We've got the office visit arranged for this morning and can do the deal on Monday. You're perfectly safe. Nothing's going to happen in Cambridge."

C.J. rocked back in his chair, nodded and smiled. "I did two tours in Iraq and in Texas, where I come from, we don't do 'runnin away."

"Good," said Simon. "If you're ready, let's get this show on the road."

C.J. Hunt stepped out of the car and looked at the glass fronted office building on the far side of the plaza. "So this is Harland Digital."

"Before we go in can I remind you about the confidentiality agreement," said Simon. "No announcement's been made to the staff."

"Don't worry," said C.J. "We won't blow your cover. You know... We have done this before."

They walked across the plaza, avoiding the water splashing from the fountain. Simon swiped his security tag. Automatic doors opened.

The two storey atrium was a riot of plants and smelt green, fragrant like a freshly watered florists.

"Pretty fancy set up," said Nico.

"Thanks," said Simon and acknowledged the receptionist with a nod. "I'll give you a royal tour. We'll start downstairs with the commercial offices, staff restaurant, crèche and the bat caves. Then I'll take you upstairs to where the magic happens - where the programmers work."

"So this is where Regis was written," said Nico.

"Our database software, that's right," said Simon. "We developed Regis here."

"Did you just say 'bat caves'?" asked Fripp.

Simon nodded. "That's right. They're quiet rooms for chilling out and thinking. No computers, no phones. Anyone can use them."

They moved slowly through the building.

Nico stopped by a tattooed girl with a line of studs in each ear, working with three computer screens. "Hey! I like your body art... Cool. What'd you do here, Honey?"

"I'm in the blue team. My job's to analyse log data using the event management platform. Right now I'm writing a programme to detect live intrusions and to triage alarms in real-time."

"So you're here to defend Regis from hackers. That's good." Nico looked at the screens. "How long you worked here?"

"Just over a year."

"Straight from college, Huh? What's your name?"

"Warwick University," replied the girl. "My name's Lauren."

"Good to meet you Lauren." She patted Lauren's hand. "I'm Nico. We're 'gona get along fine."

Lauren looked at the group gathered around her workstation. "Are you going to be working with us?"

"Sure we're..."

Simon cut her short. "Time for coffee. Thanks Lauren." He smiled at the programmer and shepherded the Americans away.

The boardroom, spartan and uncluttered, was on the corner of the building, overlooking the plaza.

"Did Neville answer your due diligence questions?" asked Simon.

"Neville, your lawyer? Sure," replied Fripp. "We're working through his reply."

"Is there a problem?"

"Nah. It's just procedure," said Fripp and reached across the table for another muffin.

After eating the party drove to Darwin College. Simon led the way to the back of the college, where a punt was padlocked to a jetty. He unlocked the mooring ring and invited the Americans aboard.

C.J. stepped awkwardly into the punt, almost capsizing it. "Geez, this thing's 'gonna sink." He settled himself, filling the front seat.

The others boarded the unsteady craft and sat down; Simon on the bow, the other Americans mid-ships. They followed the river past Queen's College. Tourists, enjoying the warm sunshine, lined the banks. An Asian family in an overloaded punt sat broadside across the river, their pole sticking upright from the water tantalisingly beyond reach. The children were giggling as their father stretched in vain to reach it.

"It isn't funny," he shouted. "Stop laughing."

People gathered on the bank to enjoy the spectacle.

John Hume nudged the Asian punt, pushing it towards the lost pole.

"Thank you. You are most kind," shouted the man recovering his composure.

"Thank you," parroted his children.

"John is going to punt us downstream to give you a good view of the colleges," explained Simon.

"That's Trinity College," said John Hume, pointing to the left bank. "Trinity is one of the biggest landowners in Britain. Trinity's our landlord. It built the science park. They say, the college owns over eight hundred million pounds of assets."

"That's a lot of dough for a college," said C.J.

A boat, loaded with students crabbed, splashing the big

American. "Sorry," called one of the girls on board.

"Lord Byron, the poet, was a student at Trinity. He kept a bear as a pet while he..."

"'Allahu Akbar."

There was a scream. A man, on the riverbank, clutched his chest, stumbled and toppled into the river. A hooded youth was running away.

John Hume sank the pole into the riverbed and drove the punt towards the man.

Simon grabbed him. "He's too heavy. C.J. give me a hand."

They turned the stricken man face up and held him against the side of the boat.

"He's too heavy to pull aboard. We'll capsize. Push for the bank," ordered Simon.

They landed and dragged the man ashore.

"He's alive. Looks like a stab wound, to me," said C.J. pulling the man's shirt open. "We need to slow the bleeding. Simon, press your hand here."

A woman was on her knees. "David... DAVID!"

"Is he your friend?" asked Simon.

"He's my husband. Why? Why did he do it?"

The wounded man clutched at his chest and whimpered.

A female police officer ran over. "What's happened?"

"He's been stabbed," said Simon. "Get an ambulance."

"Move back," shouted the police woman. "Give us some room." She radioed for assistance.

A man pushed his way through the crowd. "I'm a doctor." He knelt, examined the wound and looked at Simon. "Was he a friend of yours?"

Simon shook his head. "That's his wife."

"No," she shrieked. "NO!"

No one spoke as Simon drove the Americans back to their hotel. "I need a drink," he said. A television above the bar was showing the BBC news channel. There was no sound but subtitles were tracking across the screen.

"It was an unprovoked attack," said presenter. The barman turned up the sound. "The attacker, identified as black and in his twenties yelled, 'Allahu Akbar,' before stabbing his victim and running off. He was later cornered and shot dead by police marksmen. Police sources say his identity is known but they will not yet be releasing a name until later."

Video, recorded on a mobile phone, showed the victim being carried to the ambulance. An interview of a witness followed. "The man and woman were walking in front of me. They were holding hands. A bloke ran up to them shouted something and hit the man in the chest. I didn't see the knife ..."

"Turn it off," snapped Simon.

"That was interesting," said Nico, sipping her beer. "Your cops are so polite. The guy who interviewed me was a real cutie. He offered to buy me dinner."

"What did you say?" asked C.J.

"I said I'd love to honey but you're not my type." She grinned. "Mind you, I was tempted."

C.J. snorted and spilt his drink. "Hell."

The barman handed him a cloth to dab his wet shirt.

John Hume joined them. "Have you heard?" He said excitedly. "The Prime Minister's resigned. Parliament's been dissolved. There's going to be a general election."

"Resigned! On a Saturday?" said Simon.

"Do you think Roberts will get in?" asked John.

"I hope so," said Simon. "We need someone to take charge and get a grip of things."

"Roberts, he's the new guy who wants to deport all the illegals," said C.J. "The President tried that back home and now he's a busted flush."

"Yes but your Mexicans are busy cutting everyone's grass and working their socks off, not blowing themselves up and killing people," said Simon. "I think Max Roberts is tough enough to sort things out. At least he has a plan."

"You really think his protocols will work?" asked John.

"Protocols! They were talking about them again on the news this morning. What exactly are protocols?" asked C.J.

"New laws Roberts says will protect the people," explained Simon. "They make a lot of sense."

"Madness more like," said John Hume. "He's a fascist. Britain will be a police state,"

The barman who had been listening to the conversation handed a copy of the evening paper to C.J. "Here," he said and pointed to the banner headline;

JABBING YOU TO FIGHT TERRORISTS
Proposed Law Sparks Fiery Row
By Chief Reporter Jason Downes

Every adult in Britain may be compelled to undergo minor surgery, with multi-purpose microchips being embedded in their arms, under new laws offered by the National People's Party.

They will monitor everyone's movements and will eventually be capable of manipulating behaviour.

This draconian move to fight terrorism is being promoted by National People's Party leader Max Roberts.

And documents leaked exclusively to Daily News confirm that this may be just a launch-pad for the most startlingly controversial legislation ever visualised in this country.

Criticisms about the 'shattering of civil liberties' – and claims that the multi-billion-pound scheme is 'Fascist lunacy' -- were contemptuously dismissed last night by Roberts.

Labour Party Chairman, Colin Walters, slams Roberts' plan as 'Orwellian and delusional.'

Roberts hit back. "We must know where the jihadists are. I'm sick of liberal lefties whinging about rights. Ask the victims of last week's attacks about their rights. Ask their families. So we all have to have a tiny microchip in our arm. So what? It doesn't hurt. The only ones who should worry are the killers and they have no rights."

Above the headline was a picture of a triumphant, Churchillian looking Max Roberts and a smaller second photograph of a microchip compared in size with a grain of rice.

C.J. turned the page. "It says here he's going to create a national database of everyone's DNA. This Roberts guy's got the right idea." C.J. returned the paper to the barman. "I'd vote for him."

"What are the plans for tomorrow?" asked Nico.

"I thought you would like to see a rugby match?" said John. "I've got tickets for the Wales - England match at Twickenham. We'll drive down in the morning."

"Rugby! Why not? Isn't that like American football?" asked C.J.

Simon laughed. "The balls are the same shape but players don't wear body armour and the game doesn't take four hours. You'll enjoy it. I'm only sorry I can't come with you."

"You can count me out, too" said Ben Fripp. "I have work to do."

"How do you think it went," asked John Hume as they left the hotel.

"Pretty well," said Simon. "Except when Nico was talking to Lauren... She nearly said something... Did you hear?"

Hume didn't answer.

"You like her don't you."

"She's a looker if that's what you mean and yes I would," said Hume, "given the chance."

They were at the car.

"Not much hope of that," said Simon. "You didn't spot it did you?.. She was making eyes at Lauren. Get in. I'll give you a lift home."

CHAPTER 4

It was after midnight when Simon got back to his flat. A light flashed on the answer phone. "Simon, it's Neville Phillips. Everything's ready for the completion meeting on Monday afternoon. We'll do it at my offices. I've emailed the Americans to confirm and suggested a five o'clock start. Oh! Another thing, I don't know if it's important but have they said anything to you about the U.S. patent rights?"

Simon deleted the message. What did Neville mean, U.S. patent rights? The Americans hadn't said a word. Was there a problem? The message was timed at half past two, ten hours ago. It was too late to ring back. Neville wouldn't appreciate being woken.

Simon lay in bed and reflected on the rehearsal Neville had insisted on for the completion meeting. A few papers to sign, warranties to give, bank accounts to change, loans to repay, a consultancy deal to agree, a formal handover and the sale would be complete. Harland Digital would belong to Systron Security. The practice had seemed straightforward. Soon Simon would be free; free to get on with his life, to spend time finding out who he really was. But, he wasn't free yet and he felt nervous. He wasn't expecting problems. The Americans were friendly enough. C.J. the C.E.O. and Nico were great, fun to be with. But the lawyer, Fripp, was different. He was a cold fish. He seldom spoke and, for some reason, Simon disliked him. Yes, if there was going to be a problem, Fripp would be the grit in the deal.

Simon remembered what Joy had said on the phone. "There were more questions from their legal team." Why hadn't he asked what the questions were? Distracted by his parent's death, Simon had taken his eye off the ball. He got up, poured himself a large whisky and turned in.

There were more terror attacks during the night. A fanatic crashed a van into worshippers outside a Birmingham mosque killing three and maiming others. The van stalled. The driver was dragged from the vehicle and beaten by the angry crowd. A mob rampaged through Forest Gate, London overturning cars and throwing petrol bombs. Police dispersed the rioters with tear gas and rubber bullets.

Simon woke early, dressed in an old tee-shirt and jeans and drove straight to the office. An armoured car was parked at the science park entrance. Soldiers, their weapons cradled across their chests, idly watched him approach. A policemen stepped from behind the vehicle and held up his arm. Simon stopped and wound his window down.

"And where are you going at six o'clock in the morning?" asked to policeman.

"Harland Digital. Over there." Simon pointed.

"On a Sunday. That's odd isn't it?" The policemen opened the car door. "Step out of the car."

Simon got out.

The officer spun him round and pushed him against the car. "Put your hands on the roof and keep them there," he ordered. He started to pat Simon down. "Is there anything sharp in your pockets?"

"No," snapped Simon.

"Is this your car?"

"Of course it's my car. Look in my back pocket. There's some identification."

The policemen pulled a wallet out and opened it revealing Simon's security pass. He studied the photograph.

"Mr. Simon Reece, Managing Director, Harland Digital." His tone changed. "I see, Sir." He handed it back and stepped away from the car. "Thank you. Sorry to have detained you."

"Is that it? You manhandle me like a criminal. You wouldn't have done that if I'd shaved and worn a suit." Simon got in the car and started the engine.

"A word of advice..."

"This isn't a police state. Not yet," snarled Simon and drove off.

He spent the morning reading the answers to the due diligence enquiries from Systron Security's lawyers. Everything looked fine. There was only one mention of patents for Regis Software and it looked harmless enough. He turned on Joy's computer, searching for the email she'd told him about on the phone. He scrolled down. There it was.

From John Wardman - Wardman Fripp Associates
To Simon Reece Harland Digital

Private and Confidential
Thank you for replying to our due diligence enquiries. Having reviewed your answers, our client has asked us to examine the international patent position for Harland Digital's Regis Software. Can you please forward all relevant documentation so that we may expedite same.

Signed John Wardman
Attorney at Law

Simon had already answered hundreds of due diligence questions about human resources, the company's tax position, property, legal issues, personal guarantees, contingent liabilities and more The Americans had fired a continuous barrage of questions. Why, at the eleventh hour as the deal was about to be signed, was their lawyer asking for paperwork dealing with international patents? It was a loose end. What were the Americans up to? Simon phoned John Hume. "How's it going?"

"We're in Twickenham walking towards the stadium," replied Hume above a babble of background chatter.

"Should be a good game," said Simon. "It might be an idea to explain how the game's played. Can I have a quick word with C.J?"

"Hi Simon," said C.J. "What's up?"

"Can I ask you something C.J? Is there a problem with our deal?"

"How 'du mean?"

"Our patents for Regis? Your lawyers in the USA have been asking for more information."

"Yea. I heard. It's nothing to worry about. Everything's fine."

Simon sighed. "So the deal's being signed tomorrow like we agreed? No tricks."

"Tricks? Simon we're here to do a deal with you."

"That's great C.J. Enjoy the game. I'll see you tomorrow."

Phillips, Tate and Shrive's Cambridge law practice was a modern, glass fronted building on Station Road. Simon and John Hume were taken up to the fourth floor and shown into the room where the deal would be done. The Americans had arrived early for the completion meeting and were seated at a large walnut table. A full-length window filled one wall, the others rich with walnut panelling. Despite facing north, the room was warm and smelt of lemon and polish. An oil painting, a judge in wig and robes, illuminated by a brass picture light, dominated the wall opposite the window.

Simon sat between Neville Phillips and John Hume.

Across the table from Simon, C.J. Systron's C.E.O. relaxed and leaned back in his chair. "You already know Nico and Ben Fripp." He gestured to his associates and pointed to two strangers, a large man with a paunch and a thin chisel faced man, seated by the window. "Frank Jacob. Frank's our software specialist. Nico's asked Frank to do some checks for us and John Wardman. John's part of our legal team. Flew in this morning."

"Welcome to Cambridge," said Simon. "You must be tired after your flight. What did you think of the rugby?"

"Hell," said C.J. "It was a tough game. Those guys play rough."

"Shall we make a start?" suggested Neville Phillips. "There's a lot to get through." He picked up agendas from the stack of papers, in the centre of the table and passed them round. "The first item is for the existing shareholders to sign stock transfer forms." He handed documents to Simon and John. "If you could just sign where I've put the pencil marks."

"Just a minute," interrupted C.J. "A couple of things have come up. John'll explain."

The chisel-faced man smiled and cleared his throat. "Thanks C.J. My search of patent filings has exposed a weakness in your American rights. The patent for Regis Software could be challenged in the US. If the patent was shot down it would have a material effect on the value of your company. I'm not saying there will be a challenge but it's a risk we have to allow for." He sat back, waiting for a reaction.

Simon looked at C.J. The Texan returned a blank stare. "You said a couple of things C.J. What's the second?"

"I'll answer that," said Nico. She sat forward and looked over the top of her glasses. "I asked Frank to do some penetration testing of Regis and I'm sorry to say your software's not secure."

"Not secure! What do you mean?" snapped John Hume.

"Frank found Regis vulnerable to attack. It's not bullet proof."

"That's a lie," replied John Hume angrily. "We've got the best coders in the world. There's nothing wrong with Regis."

"Easy John, let's hear them out," said Simon, putting his hand on John 's arm. "I take it Frank's specialisation is cyber security?" Frank nodded.

"How did you do the pen test?"

"Go ahead Frank," said Nico.

"OK. I tested with a Neutrino Exploit Kit and then did some manual stuff but it wasn't a full security audit."

"You hacked our system with malicious software without telling us!" shouted John.

"Frank Jacob shrugged. "It's what I'm paid to do and.." he smiled, "one of the dumbest ways in was laterally." He looked at John. "I accessed Harland's system through your home computer."

John Hume stood up and glared at Jacob. "You hacked my home computer!"

"Relax John," said C.J. He was smiling now, enjoying John Hume's discomfort. "Sit down. Don't worry. Harland Digital is a great business and we want Regis Software. Like I told Simon yesterday we're here to do a deal. Systron still want to do the deal. But you must appreciate our position."

"I thought the deal was agreed," said Simon. "We've been together for two days and you've said nothing. Not a word about the patent or Regis software... I even asked you if there was a problem. Remember? And you," he pointed at Fripp, "said 'no, everything was fine'."

Simon paused. "So what is your position?"

Ben Fripp answered. "We have two proposals. The first is that Harland's directors, give personal guarantees the

U.S. patents will hold up if challenged. I've prepared draft undertakings." He passed a paper across the table to Neville Phillips.

The lawyer studied it. "It says here, unlimited and without time constraint."

"What does that mean?" asked Simon.

"It means the guarantee is for every penny paid for the business and is for everything you and John have and there is no time limit. You would be underwriting the future success of Harland Digital for ever."

"Look at it from our point of view," said C.J. "We're trying to help you out here. Systron Security agreed eight million for Harland Digital. That's a great deal of money and we're still willing to pay but we need some comfort that what we're buying isn't a crock of crap."

"Some comfort," spat Simon. "We'd be wedded to the business for all time. Waiting for the day you come back and put your hand in our pockets. What's the other offer?"

"OK. We are willing to take all the risk," replied Fripp. "And it's a big risk, but it would reflect on the price,"

"So, at the last minute after saying nothing to warn us, you're reducing your offer! HOW MUCH?" demanded Simon glaring at Fripp.

"Don't get angry, Simon," said C.J. "Hell. This is business."

Fripp produced another document. "I've drafted a revised share sale agreement showing the consideration we're willing to pay." He passed the papers across the table.

Simon snatched them and flicked to the last page. He showed it to John Hume. "WHAT," shouted John. "You're taking the piss. This is a bloody joke."

"It's no joke," replied Fripp. "It's a serious offer to buy Harland Digital."

"And what if we say no?" shouted Simon. He thrust the paper towards Neville.

John Wardman, replied. "Systron could challenge your

patent in the Federal Courts."

Simon banged his fist on the table, "You bastards..."

Neville Phillips put his hand on Simon's arm. "Before we respond, my side needs a break to discuss these unexpected changes, privately. Excuse us for a few minutes." He stood up and ushered Simon and John to a small office.

"Four million! An offer of four million," snorted John. "Where, the hell, did that come from?"

"Shit, shit, SHIT... We've been ambushed," said Simon. "They planned this all along. How the hell did he get in through your home computer?"

John didn't answer.

"Look," said Simon. "We all know Regis is fine. So they've pen tested. So what? There's nothing wrong with Regis software that can't be fixed."

"Maybe so," replied Neville Phillips. "But the lawyer Wardman, I looked him up. He's a lead counsel with a name. He wins big patent cases. American patent law is a minefield and it's the side with money that wins."

"The weasel's threatening us," said Simon. "Do the deal. Sell Harland for half of its value or he'll use the American legal system to screw us?"

The lawyer nodded. "Could tie you up for years. It's your call Simon. What do you want to do?"

Simon turned to John Hume. "Your ten percent share option doesn't look quite so attractive now, does it John?.. We need to buy some time. Let's go back and tell the Yanks we still think a deal is possible but we want to consider the different offers in more detail."

C.J. showed no surprise when they asked for more time. "No problem. Our plans have changed. Something's come up and we'll be staying in the UK for a few days. You boys have a think. What say we hook up in a week to settle things?" He stood up, threw a casual salute towards Simon and moved towards the door.

"We're going to need longer. A month and we need to see the results of the penetration test," answered Simon.

"A month?" The Texan stopped. "OK, one month and Frank'll send you the details of the test, but no longer. We'll come back to the UK then. One more thing. Remember this, you signed an exclusivity agreement and can't talk with any other potential buyers while we're still negotiating. My legal boys here would be VERY UPSET if they learned you were going behind our backs."

CHAPTER 5

Simon was at work the following day when his phone rang. There was a courier downstairs who refused to leave a delivery without seeing him. The man was insistent. Simon Reece must sign for the box marked private and confidential. He waited in reception until Simon came down.

"What do you think it is? Looks like a ream of paper," said Simon as he scribbled on the courier's tablet.

The courier grabbed the tablet and hurried out.

Simon took the parcel up to his office, shut the door and un-wrapped it. I contained a letter.

Dear Mr. Reece,

Your organisation, Harland Digital, along with others, is invited to offer a tender for provision of a new national DNA database, to the specification outlined in the attached documents. Enclosed are:

Document 1   Instructions and information on the tendering procedures.
Document 2   Specification of the Requirement.
Document 3   List of attachments.

Document 4   Declaration and information to be provided by tenderer.

Please contact me if you have any questions about the tendering procedure. The enclosed Document 1 also contains details providing you with further information and clarification of the Government's requirement.

Signed
James Lucas
Home Office Second Permanent Secretary.

Simon slit open the plastic pouch. The tender documents were huge... hundreds of pages of specifications, details and conditions. Was it possible? Could Harland Digital, the company Simon started, compete and win this deal? This was a big opportunity, build a national DNA database - wow! It changed everything. Win this contract and Harland would be a major player, a massive Tech Company at the top table. Supply the government's database and selling to Systron, playing their games - arguing over patents and penetration tests would all be irrelevant.

Simon dialled the number on the letter. It was a direct line.

"You've reached James Lucas." The voice sounded young. "Leave your name and number and I'll get back to you. If the call is urgent, dial zero and you'll be put through to the switchboard."

Simon left a message and hung up.

James Lucas phoned back later that morning. "I'm glad you called. Things are moving fast. We should meet," said Lucas. "National security is at stake. Can you meet me at the River Palace this evening?"

Simon looked at his diary. He had a meeting at three o'clock. "The River Palace, where is it?"

"London. It's on the Albert Embankment. Come to the

twelfth floor. There's an executive suite with a private restaurant. I'll buy you dinner. There's valet parking. Just give your keys to the concierge. Eight o'clock."

Simon searched the Home Office website; no mention of a second permanent secretary called James Lucas - no Facebook or LinkedIn page. Google; nothing. He checked the Whitehall Civil Service List. The Home Office had several Permanent Secretaries but no Lucas. His name wasn't on the list.

Simon rang the Home Office. "James Lucas please?"

"Which department?" asked the telephonist.

"I'm not sure," replied Simon.

"I'm sorry caller. The Home Office has six ministerial departments and thousands of staff... Unless you can be specific I can't help."

"He's a Second Permanent Secretary."

"One moment..."

Simon waited.

"You've reached James Lucas." It was the same recorded message. "Leave your name and number and I'll get back to you. If the call is urgent, dial zero and your will be put through to the switchboard."

Simon cancelled his meeting, spent the morning reading the tender documents and left for London.

"Accident ahead - stationery vehicles," said the motorway gantry.

Simon checked his watch - plenty of time.

The traffic was slowing down. It stopped. An accident on the M11 blocked the motorway. Police cars and a fire engine raced along the hard shoulder. Cars and lorries crawled slowly forward. An hour passed. Simon heard a siren. An ambulance passed. Ahead flames, blue lights and carnage; overturned cars and a blazing lorry. The motorway beyond the accident was clear. Simon accelerated. A speed camera flashed. He glanced at the speedometer; a hundred and five. "Shit."

He had to hurry. Simon sped through east London. He could see the skyscrapers of Canary Wharf ahead. Good. He'd made up lost time.

The traffic stopped. The road into London was blocked. He looked at the time, twenty past seven. Now what? Cars inched towards a police line.

"What's happening?" called Simon.

"A demonstration. Road's closed," replied a policeman and pointed. "Follow the diversion."

Simon was moving slowly along Commercial Road when a bottle smashed on the bonnet of his car. Small groups of hooded youths jeered and made obscene gestures at the passing vehicles. Missiles littered the road- a battleground of bricks, broken glass, looted shops and the acrid stink of burned out cars.

Riot police waved the cars through a police barricade at Aldgate, towards central London and a different world. One protected from the rioters. Tourists were out, commuters hurrying to catch their trains, late shoppers laden with bags.

It was half past eight when Simon reached the River Palace. He threw his keys to the parking attendant and hurried into the hotel.

A concierge showed Simon the lift. He leaned in and pressed the button for the twelfth floor. "Mr. Lucas has already arrived Sir. Just tell the maître d' who you are," he said as the doors closed.

Simon stepped into a corridor of black carpeted walls, the floor covered with grey carpet, illuminated by small floor lights. The corridor turned a corner and ended at double doors leading to a comfortable executive restaurant. Panoramic windows, night views of the Thames and the Houses of Parliament added to the theatre. Fluorescent blue London Eye gondolas glowed and reflected against the inky black of the river.

"Mr. Reece? This way, Sir." The maître d' showed Simon to a table by the window. "Mr. Lucas is making a phone call. He'll join you shortly. Can I get you a drink? An aperitif perhaps?"

"A whisky and water... Tell me something. The building over there by the bridge. Is that MI5?"

"No Sir. That is MI6. MI5 is on the far bank." He pointed across the river.

A brightly lit river bus was passing under Lambeth Bridge when James Lucas arrived. The second secretary, well groomed, tall with chisel features, looked as boyish as he'd sounded. "Good, you've got a drink." He sat down. The way Lucas moved, his bearing, he was obviously fit and the way he talked, reminded Simon of a junior army officer who knew the answer to a question before it was asked.

"I'm sorry I'm late. East London was a mess."

"You came that way? I'm surprised."

"Yes and there's big dent in my bonnet. Some bastard threw a bottle at the car."

Lucas checked his phone and placed it on the table. "Simon, may I call you Simon? It's good of you to come at short notice. Things are moving more quickly than anticipated. We need to act."

A waiter arrived and handed them menus. "The specials tonight, gentlemen, are tomato and apple soup and salmon en croute. Would you like a wine list Mr. Lucas?"

Lucas nodded. "The food here is excellent. Freshly prepared and the hotel has a good wine cellar. I recommend the fillet steak with a pepper sauce and baby new potatoes."

"Sounds good," said Simon.

The second secretary ordered two steaks. "And a bottle of Caymus, the 2013 special selection."

"The Caymus Carbernet Sauvignon. Certainly, Sir and I'll bring some mineral water?"

"You've seen what it's like. Rioting in the streets. Yesterday three policemen were stabbed in Bradford. Law and order has broken down. The government has collapsed. There's no political leadership. We're heading towards civil war," said Lucas. "There's only one way to sort the mess out, to stop the insanity... You know what it is, don't you?"

"The country needs a strong leader," said Simon. "Someone with balls and an iron will who's prepared to over-rule the 'terrorists also have rights brigade'."

"Exactly. I'm glad we agree. Max Roberts will win the election with a landslide. He will be the next Prime Minister and we're preparing to implement his policies."

"How do you know Roberts will win by a landslide?"

"He will. It's the only way we can take back control," said Lucas. "Emergency legislation will be passed immediately."

"You seem very confident."

"It's what we all want, isn't it?.. You are with us?"

"Yes. I want to help," said Simon and wondered who 'us' were.

"The security situation is going to get far worse. Canary Wharf was the target this afternoon... anti capitalists."

The maître d' approached. "Is everything satisfactory gentlemen?"

Lucas nodded and waved him away. "We have intelligence that the attacks are a precursor, designed to incite racial hatred and spark a war. Tonight there's going to be a demonstration in Hackney and rent a mob will be there. The country's on a knife edge. We are going to act." The second secretary sat back in his chair.

Simon swallowed a mouthful. "Who do you really work for? You're not from the Home Office. Are you a spook?"

Lucas laughed. "A spook! Nothing so exciting. I work for the Home Office." He checked his phone then studied Simon for a moment. "Can your company do what we're asking?"

"Yes. I'm confident we can. Integration of the DNA database with NHS records, the DVLA, Revenue and Customs, criminal records and the other databases is a massive project. We'll need to do some rewriting of the programme but Regis will do all the linking and pinning. There is part of the tender that's not clear."

"And what is that?"

" How you will track the chip implants. Regis can't do that."

Lucas refilled his glass. "Don't worry. We'll supply the control codes for everything. You'll get the technical details once a contract has been signed."

Simon knew he was being fobbed off. "I do have other questions. You're entering the realm of guarded personal information. Who will have access? What about false positive matches? We've already seen that problem with the American no-fly lists, innocent people being turned off aeroplanes."

"Yes. We've thought of that. They're all issues that need addressing," replied Lucas. "As for false positives, they will happen." He shrugged. "It's a price that will have to be paid. Call it necessary collateral damage if you like."

Simon nodded. "How many companies are tendering?"

"I'm not at liberty to say but I will tell you this. There is one other serious contender for the project, an American company and, off the record. I think the Americans might not be reliable... Dessert?" asked Lucas. He beckoned to a waiter. "Bring Mr. Reece a menu."

The waiter hurried away and returned with the menu.

Simon chose the cheeseboard. "What are you having?"

"I'm not a pudding man." Lucas patted his stomach. "No good for the figure."

Simon drove back to Cambridge with mixed feelings. This was a fantastic opportunity for Harland Digital but at the same time, he had doubts. The enormity of consolidating dozens of different databases was possible but it would be an enormous task. Regis was capable of doing the work but they would need to recruit a bigger team and fast. There was a lot to think about. Not least the dangers of what was planned. It would give the state, or whoever else controlled the data, a weapon of immense power. With it came total control not just of persons of interest to the security services but of every human being in the land. At the press of a button the authorities would know, at any time, exactly where anyone was, where they had been and who they were associating with.

Was this the way forward for a modern democracy or, as John Hume had said, the beginning of an Orwellian super state where a person's rights and civil liberties were sacrificed when necessary? "Collateral damage," James Lucas had called it.

Despite his reservations, the decision to go after the deal was already made. Harland needed the contract. Simon wanted it and if necessary was prepared to be, 'One of us'.

Calling his management team together Simon warned them the tender was to remain secret not to be discussed with anyone. He stressed how important the contract was to the future success of the business, divided the work up and set a deadline. It was critical. Harland's proposal must be ready in seven days. It was an almost impossible task.

On the second day John Hume walked into Simon's office and threw the tender on his desk. "It can't be done."

Simon looked up from his computer. "What's wrong?"

"You said a week to produce a proposal. Never mind a bloody week. I can't even work out if it's possible. Could take months, years even with the team we have."

"John, you're not making any sense... Sit down and tell me what the problem is."

"It's the specification." Hume jabbed an accusing finger at the tender document on Simon's desk. "There on page eighty-seven, the two way communication. We can't do what they want. You said you'd read it."

Simon turned to page eighty-seven. "I didn't see that."

"For fuck's sake Simon. Regis isn't a command and

control system. It's designed for data capture and analysis."

Simon got up and shut the door. "So what if it's going to take more time to write the programme. We'll do that later. We'll recruit more programmers. Don't you see?.." He sat down in a chair opposite Hume. "Right now all we're doing is tendering for the contract. If you don't know how, guess. The details of how can be sorted later."

The technical director rubbed the back of his neck. "I don't understand what it's for. Why send signals to a passive device? The microchips are inert. They can't do anything."

What was it for? There was no explanation, in the tender document. Simon phoned Lucas and asked. "Two way communication. What's it for?"

"No idea. I'll find out and ring you back," said Lucas.

At the same time, Simon was wrestling with the vexing question of what to do about Systron Security. Their offer was ridiculous, a punt to get the price down and there was something else. If Harland Digital won the government contract, the value of the Simon's company would go through the roof. Never mind four million or eight million, potentially it would be worth ten, twenty times more possibly even more than that. The government contract, if Harland won it, changed everything. But, should he tell the Americans to get lost, risking a patent lawsuit in the US or reveal Harland was possibly about to win a huge deal?

There was another complication. Lucas had said, an American company was tendering. But who? Then Simon remembered C.J.'s parting shot; something had come up. The Americans were staying in the UK for a few days. Was the Home Office talking to Systron Security? It made sense. Systron managed data for hundred of companies and governments.

CHAPTER 6

It was after midnight when Simon got home. He stepped over letters in the hall, poured a drink and collapsed onto the sofa. Rolling the glass between his hands, he studied the rainbow of colours reflecting in the crystal.

He refilled the drink and picked up the post; junk mail and a brown envelope; a reply from the General Register Office. He hesitated then tore it open, pulled out a duplicate birth certificate and read it.

Name; Simon Frederick Jackson
Male, Date of Birth; 14th August 1978
Place of birth; Bancroft Maternity Home, Bristol
Father; William Jackson
Mother; Florence Jackson nee Wilks
Father's occupation; Mechanical Engineer
Description and residence of informant; William Jackson Coed Mawr, Pontgarreg, Ceredigion
Date of registration of birth 16th August 1978.

At last, Simon had what he needed for the Adoption Contact Register and... he had an address. He opened Google earth, typed Coed Mawr, Pontgarreg. A solitary house appeared.

He grinned. The house was near the coast - clean, white, freshly painted - a house someone was proud of. Geraniums, splurges of brilliant red, cascaded from window boxes.

Simon rummaged through his papers. The contact register letter, where was it? He found it, hurriedly scribbled the missing details in and stuffed it in an envelope. Success... Time for another drink, one more to celebrate - a nightcap. He refilled and sat, staring at the laptop.

He played absent mindedly with the keyboard and typed, 'Coed Mawr' in the search box.

A link appeared on the screen. "Holiday home gutted - two dead."

The link went to a newspaper archive page - Western Mail Newspaper 18th September 1980.

"Responsibility for the arson attack at Coed Mawr," said the article, "was claimed by Meibion Glyndwr (Sons of Glyndwr). Two people died in the blaze. William Jackson and his wife Florence. Their children, twins Simon and Pamela aged two were rescued from the smoke filled building by firemen..."

A picture showed the charred ruin of a house with soot covered walls. There were no windows, no door and no roof but the shape was the same. It was the house Simon had found on Google earth.

It was a gut wrenching blow. The euphoria of having an address, of discovering the house, bathed in sunlight, was gone smothered by disappointment. The search was over. He'd already buried one set of parents and now, when he was so close, the others had been snatched away, turned to ashes. Simon took the envelope addressed to the Adoption Register and tore it into tiny pieces. Then, he re-read the article. Twins Simon and Pamela... He had a sister.

Emlyn Hughes replaced the telephone receiver and looked

around his study. He felt good. The picture of him, holding a CBE at the palace smiled back at him, another taken when he was awarded his Queen's Police Medal, sat on the brightly polished desk. Life had been quiet for Emlyn Hughes since his retirement. He'd loved being a policeman and enjoyed the status the job gave him as he rose through the ranks. His colleagues had called him ruthless, prepared to bend the rules to get the job done, but he'd never cared. Hughes was a workaholic so rarely home that when his wife left him he hardly noticed. Obsessed with work and ambition, he soon forgot her. But now, no longer the centre of activity making decisions and giving orders, the retired Chief Constable of Dyfed-Powys Police was alone and, although he refused to admit it, lost.

He went to the kitchen, filled the kettle and made a mug of instant coffee. There was work to do. The phone call had been from an old friend, a call to action and an offer that might, just might, restore Hughes to a position of power.

Hughes returned to the study, sat at his computer, opened a new document and entered a filename. 'Director of Internal Security - Job Description.' He pressed save, swallowed a mouthful of coffee and started to type.

Simon was on the M42 when John Hume rang. "Hi John."

"Where are you?"

A tailgating car flashed its headlights. Simon accelerated to overtake a coach. "I'm on my way to Wales." He changed lanes to let the car behind pass.

"Wales, Christ... Simon our deal with Systron is about to go tits up, we suddenly have the chance of our lives and you're swanning about. I need you here."

"I know... John, don't panic. I'll be back tomorrow. We'll go through the tender then. I've got to go."

Simon stopped at Strensham services and grabbed a coffee. He was back on the road when the phone went again.

How are you buddy? It's C.J." The voice was crackly through the speaker. "Listen. I've been thinking about our meeting. John Wardman was out of order."

"I'm good C.J. What do you mean, out of order?"

"The patent thing. Sure there's an issue but we shouldn't have nailed you to the floor."

"You mean the price?"

"Yeah, the price. We'll pay eight million and forget the guarantees."

"You will. Why the change of heart?" Simon sipped coffee.

"Hell. I'm a businessman but I'm not a fool. Sure I wanted to stiff you but you're not going to cave in. I can see that."

Simon wiped his mouth and smiled. "What about the penetration tests? Your man said Regis had security issues."

C.J. laughed. "Frank says with some extra coding the software will be bullet proof so there's no reason why we can't sign the deal. Say, let's get together tomorrow. We'll meet you..." The call disconnected. Simon glanced at the Jaguar's computer screen - no phone signal.

He was at Ross on Wye when C.J. rang back.

"The phone just died. As I was saying, ring your lawyer. Tell him to set the meeting up."

"C.J. I can't."

"You can't. Godamn it! Why the hell not?"

"I'm going to Wales. Anyway, I need to talk to John."

"Call him... Wales! Where the hell is Wales? Look Simon, you'll only get one shot at this. I've already transferred eight million to a British bank and I need to get back to the States. Don't mess me about."

"Thanks for the offer C.J. It sounds good and I appreciate what you said. I'll talk to John and give you a call back. Bye." Simon hung up. It was the American's turn to stew for a while.

CHAPTER 7

Water ran down the wall, on to the path and formed a puddle between the flagstones. Sandra Tate refilled the watering can and moved to the next window box. She finished watering, replaced the watering can on a hook beside the tap and began to pick dead flower heads from the geraniums. A post office van pulled.

The driver got out. "Morning Sandra. It's not paint this time." He went to the back of the van and produced a parcel. "Feels like books."

"You know me, still learning to be an artist... It's a course about painting seascapes in any medium."

"There's plenty of sea to paint." The postman waved to the coast. "The sun's shining. The blue of the sky and the sea. Beautiful isn't it?"

A Jaguar cruised slowly along the lane and stopped behind the van.

"You've got a visitor," said the postman and drove off.

Sandra studied the driver; black hair, slightly greying temples, boyish features, fortyish, a stranger. He was holding a picture, comparing it with the house.

"Are you from the council?"

Simon got out of the car. "No... I'm not from the

council. My parents lived here once."

"Really?.. How long ago?"

"In the 1970s."

Sandra rested her parcel on the wall. "So they would have been here before the house was rebuilt."

"They were here when the house caught fire." He handed her the image of the burnt out shell.

"Oh! I'm sorry... I've never seen this before." She returned the picture. "So you've come to have a look."

"I don't really know why I've come except I needed to see the house."

"I'm Sandra Tate." She offered a hand. "Come in and have a look."

They drank coffee while Simon told her his story.

"Wow! I knew the house had been rebuilt but your picture. It was gutted. I bought Coed Mawr in 2009."

"Did you know people died in the fire?" asked Simon.

"Yes of course," replied Sandra. "That's why I got a good deal... I'm sorry. That was insensitive of me."

"It doesn't matter. I was two at the time so I don't remember anything of the fire."

"But you lost your Mum and Dad; your whole family - gone in an instant."

Simon stood up and went to the window. "Not quite. I had a sister, Pamela, she survived." He looked across the field to the sea beyond, blue and inviting. He felt confused and empty. Nothing here helped. He'd invited himself into a stranger's home, Sandra's home, into her kitchen, comfortable and warm. There was no trace of a fire, no burnt embers or clues to follow.

"Are you alright?"

"I'm really don't know why I came?" Simon turned to face Sandra. "There's nothing here for me. I have no memory of the house, of my sister, my parents - nothing"

"Did you come because you want to find your sister, to find out who did it?"

He smiled. "Thanks."

"What for?" Sandra stood up. "Drink your coffee. I'll show you the rest of the house."

She showed him round. "...and this is my studio," she said as they went upstairs. The geranium framed window faced the sea. Unfinished canvasses leaned haphazardly against walls. The room smelt of oils, turpentine and sea air. A half painted scene, yachts racing with billowing sails and cliffs stood on an easel.

"Yours?.. It's very good."

"No it isn't." Sandra blushed. "It's a daub. The sea's not right. I've got the sailing boats but the water looks flat... lifeless. There's no movement." She covered the painting with a sheet.

They'd finished the tour and Simon was leaving when Sandra suddenly said, "I'd like to help. I could ask around. There may be someone in the village who knew your parents."

Returning to Cambridge, Simon got stuck behind a slow moving army convoy with no chance of passing. The convoy stopped outside Raglan to allow traffic to pass. His phone rang.

"Simon, Beverley Manning from Parker and Smith, estate agents. Good news. I've got an offer on the house."

"That was quick. How much?"

"It's an old couple, cash buyers. There's no chain and they're willing to pay the asking price; two hundred and twenty thousand. Best of all they're in rented accommodation and want to move quickly."

Simon eased the Jaguar past the last army lorry and accelerated. "That is good news. How quickly?"

"They want to move within three weeks, when their lease expires."

"I'm not sure we can do that. There's been no inquest and I haven't got probate yet.... I'll tell you what... Explain the situation and tell them they can move in and rent the house until we can complete the deal."

"OK, I'll offer them a short term rental agreement with a purchase option," suggested Beverley. "I don't think there will be a problem. They are genuine people and that way your back's covered."

Emlyn Hughes re-read the job description, corrected a typo and emailed the document to the National People's Party executive office.

That evening Max Roberts called him. "I've read your email. It looks fine. Emlyn, I need someone loyal who I can trust implicitly. The Office of Internal Security will have complete control of the nation's security apparatus and will report direct to me. All other services, the police, the intelligence services including military intelligence will answer to the OIS..." he paused. "The job of director is yours but there will be no public announcement until after the election."

Hughes smiled, "As I see it this country needs a revolution to bring it to its senses but there will be casualties. For the protocols to work, I'll need full authority to act without anyone second guessing or getting in my way."

"Naturally and you will have it," replied Roberts. "It's good to have you with me Emlyn. It'll be like old times. There's something else. I need you to watch my back. As we move forward some NPP members might get upset and say, 'We're going too far.' They will need dealing with."

"You can rely on me, Max. I won't let you down."

"Good. You need to get started. Your Deputy Director is already at work. His name's Lucas, James Lucas. He's young, bright and committed to the cause. You'll work well together. I'll tell him to call you."

Confirmation that Harland had won the contract to provide the new national database came ten days before the election. Lucas called saying he wanted his own people installed in Harland's offices immediately, as the tender documents stipulated and there was a new condition. The government would be licensing Regis software to Systron Security for use in the United States of America.

"Why should you give my software to the Americans?" demanded Simon. "It doesn't make sense."

"To be blunt, it stops you getting sued for patent infringement. I'm doing you a favour," replied Lucas. "And... Giving Regis to the Americans gives us a back door to their records."

"Have you discussed this with Systron?"

"Of course not," replied Lucas. "But I met C.J. Hunt yesterday to agree the terms of the licensing deal."

Lucas was playing both companies at the same time; negotiating with C.J. Hunt behind Simon's back. That was why C.J. had phoned trying to buy Harland Digital for the original asking price, why the American had been so excited, so apologetic about his lawyer's threats; he wanted Harland Digital's Regis software to do his own deal with James Lucas.

"What if I refuse to license Regis to Systron?"

"That would be a big mistake, Simon. Britain is facing a national emergency and the government will take whatever steps necessary. National security over-rides all other considerations. With us or not, the Americans will get Regis. You're getting paid handsomely and we get what we need. Everyone's happy."

The licensing contract was signed the following day.

As predicted by Lucas, the result of the election was a landslide. The NPP won more than seventy percent of the vote. Max Robert was the new Prime Minister. Returning from the palace, he stood on the steps of Number 10 and declared Britain was entering a new era; a time when law and order would be restored. "Terrorists will be hunted down and dealt with. No longer will the people be at the mercy of cowards who bomb and maim. We have the technology and the weapons to root them out, to destroy them."

"Prime Minister," shouted a female news correspondent, "Will you be suspending habeas corpus?"

Roberts turned and went into his new Downing Street home. The door closed behind him.

The correspondent turned to camera. "So the new Prime Minister is making dealing with terrorism his first priority and he's not hanging around. A source tells me that legislation creating a new security organisation will be put before parliament and the national DNA database, we've heard so much about, will go live within weeks. That, of course, raises questions of human rights. Are you happy to be on the new database when you've done nothing wrong? Earlier, I asked some members of the public how they felt about it. Here's what they had to say." The reporter smiled, until the cameraman gave her a thumbs up signal, then she removed her earpiece and switched off the microphone. "What do you think Tom? Are you happy to be on the new database?" She pushed the dead microphone under the cameraman's nose.

"Um, it's marvellous, Mr. Roberts is an um wonderful um man. He's going to get all the bad guys and um save us all," replied the cameraman mockingly. They started to laugh.

"Bugger this," said the reporter. "I'm getting cold standing here. Nothing's going to happen for a while. Let's go and get a drink."

Distant sirens warned of oncoming emergency vehicles. Cars pulled over. Pedestrians craned their necks to see as a squad of police motorcycle outriders escorted two cars through the busy London streets. Some rode ahead of the cars to stop traffic, others behind. The motorcade, a black Range Rover followed by a dark blue armoured Bentley, was travelling at speed. From Hyde Park, it sped south along Grosvenor Place, past Victoria Station, scattering a rush hour phalanx of commuters emerging from the underground. The convoy continued along Vauxhall Bridge Road, turned into Gillingham Street and slowed. An electric gate slid open and, without stopping, the convoy disappeared into the bowels of a tall nondescript office block.

A security guard stepped forward and opened the Bentley's door. Emlyn Hughes stepped out of the car and shook hands with James Lucas, his new deputy.

"Good morning Director," said Lucas. "It's good to see you again. I'll take you up to your office. It's on the top floor."

A lift whisked them to the 23rd floor. The doors opened onto the executive suite of the Office for Internal Security. Tradesmen were installing a reception area and fitting office partitions. Others were installing workstations. Electricians were busy laying cabling and communications wiring. The rooms buzzed with activity. The director's suite, on the south side of the building was quieter. Hughes stood surveying the panorama; the curve of the river, the dome of Tate Britain and the brutal lines of the MI6 building on the far bank. A woman arrived with a tray of coffee and placed it on a low table between a pair of rich leather sofas. The OIS's new director went over to an ornate desk, sat down and positioned a framed picture, of himself being presented his medal by the Queen, on a shelf. Dissatisfied, he moved the picture to the corner of his desk where it was easier for visitors to see. He smiled and motioned for Lucas to sit. "James, have the orders for the DNA capture programme been prepared as I instructed?"

"They have Director. The television campaign starts next week followed by individual notices instructing people where to go to be swabbed."

"And the database. When will it be ready?"

"It's already live but a work in progress. It'll take time to consolidate the information from all the different sources. We can start adding the DNA data as soon as it's available but it will take six months, maybe more, before the information is comprehensive and reliable."

"Six months," snorted the director. "Ridiculous! I want it done sooner."

"Programming and testing the code to connect and cross check innumerable sets of data for seventy million people takes time, director."

A phone on the desk rang. It was the Prime Minister's office. Max Roberts was put through. "Emlyn, congratulations. I want to see you at Downing Street this evening. Come for dinner at eight," he ordered. "We have a lot to discuss."

CHAPTER 8

Harland Digital went into overdrive after the election. An OIS management team moved in. Officers with Lucas' authority meddled in every aspect of the new database. Lucas wanted immediate results. He demanded the impossible dismissing the complexity of what they were attempting. It was crazy. Communication broke down. A toxic atmosphere spread through the company demoralising everyone.

Simon resented the interference and was beginning to doubt the wisdom of the project. The OIS was building a machine to monitor and control the population; a weapon of immense power, which could be used for good or evil.

"We need more time," said Simon. "And you have to ease off."

"No. Your programmers need to pull their fingers out," shouted Lucas. "I'm beginning to think your people are deliberately delaying."

Simon was summoned to London, to OIS headquarters to explain the lack of progress to the director, Emlyn Hughes.

Hughes ushered Simon to a sofa by the window and sat opposite him. He poured himself a coffee and sipped it.

"My deputy tells me you're falling behind with the programme," said Hughes casually. "That it won't be ready on time."

"He's demanding miracles. We're delivering to the original programming plan but you keep adding new requirements and insisting the work be done faster. What you're asking is impossible."

"Impossible! Nothing is impossible Mr. Reece with the right commitment and motivation." The director studied Simon. He stood up. "It was good to meet you Mr. Reece. Thank you for coming. Lucas will show you out."

Simon arrived for work early the following morning. He held his pass to the scanner and pushed the door. It didn't move. He tried again. Nothing - the door was still locked. He pressed the intercom.

"Can I help you?" asked a voice.

"It's Simon. Can you unlock the door? My pass isn't working."

"I'm sorry Mr. Reece, you don't have security clearance."

"What! Don't be ridiculous. Open the door."

The young programmer, Lauren arrived. "Morning Simon." She fumbled in her bag, produced her pass and swiped it. The lock clicked open. Simon held the door and followed her into the atrium. There was a shout. He dodged a guard and sprinted upstairs to his office. James Lucas was sitting at Simon's desk.

"What the hell's going on?"

"I was just telling Joy," said Lucas.

"Telling her what?"

Lucas looked at Joy. "Give us a moment."

"Is it true?" asked Joy. "You've resigned?"

"No I bloody well haven't."

Men were running along the corridor. A security team burst in.

"I'm sorry Sir. He sneaked in," said one.

"Your resignation was confirmed by Director Hughes last night." Lucas was smiling. "Show Mr. Reece out."

The security men grabbed Simon and marched him out. John Hume was on the stairs.

"John, the bastard Lucas has fired me."

John Hume averted his eyes and kept walking.

"John. DID YOU KNOW?"

Simon struggled to break free. A punch winded him. They dragged him from the building. "Turn him round," said a voice. A fist smashed against his face. He crumpled and fell.

A gorilla of a man bent down. He ripped Simon's pass from its neck-strap, stepped back and kicked Simon in the chest.

Simon didn't move. The guards walked way. Above them, in the upstairs windows, silent faces watched then melted away. The spectacle was over.

No one came to help Simon. He sat up and wiped blood from his face. His body ached. He pulled himself up, staggered back to his car and rested his head against the steering wheel.

His phone rang. "Are you alright?" asked Lauren. "I saw what they did."

"I've been better," mumbled Simon.

"I tried to come out but they wouldn't let me. They've locked the doors. What will you do?"

Simon didn't answer.

"I'm sorry... I've got to go. Someone's coming..." The line went dead.

Simon parked in a side street. He needed to think. A woman pushing a baby buggy walked slowly along the pavement. Behind her a little girl, four or five, stamped her foot and refused to move. The woman turned and slapped the girl on the back of her leg. The child started to cry but still would not move. The woman hit her again, harder this time. The girl screamed, a piercing cry of pain. The woman seized the girl's arm, dragged her to the buggy and strapped her in. The child fought back, twisting writhing to stay free, but was no match for the woman. Simon watched them turn the corner and disappear.

"I'll fight the bastards," muttered Simon. He drove to Station Road and hurried into the offices of Phillips, Tate and Shrive.

"I need to see Neville Phillips. Tell him It's Simon Reece."

The receptionist looked at him strangely as she relayed the message.

"Mr. Phillips will be down shortly," said the girl. "The bathroom's over there. You've got blood on you."

Simon went to the toilet and splashed water on his face.

Neville Phillips was in reception when he returned. "Good God Simon. What's happened?"

"I was thrown out of my own company by some goons."

The solicitor took Simon to a meeting room and shut the door.

"Neville, I need help. I've been sacked from Harland."

"Sacked, but it's your company. I don't understand... Who sacked you?"

"Lucas, no it wasn't Lucas. It was Hughes."

"The Director of the OIS?"

Simon nodded.

"I see," said Phillips. "That puts me in a difficult position. I can't give you any legal advice."

"Neville - You're my lawyer."

"I'm afraid not Simon. You see, when you instructed me you were the Managing Director of Harland Digital and my instructions were to act on behalf of the company. There's a conflict of interest. I can't litigate or advise you against the company."

"So you won't help me?"

"I can't, but I will give you one piece of advice. Don't

challenge the OIS. They'll destroy you."

"...And that's all you have to say." Simon stood up. "You're a bloody coward."

Simon threw his visitor's badge towards the reception desk as he left. It missed and landed on the floor.

Phillips picked up the badge and handed it to his receptionist. "If Mr. Reece calls again tell him I'm in meetings."

He watched Simon stride to his car, rip a parking ticket from the windscreen and throw it in the gutter.

Simon was dozing in an armchair when the telephone rang. The room was dark. He reached for the receiver, knocking over a bottle.

"Simon! It's Joy."

A stabbing pain jolted Simon awake. A glass tumbler, wedged against the seat, was digging into his wet leg. He switched on a table lamp. The incandescent glare hurt. He shielded his eyes. A bottle lay on the table in a pool of whisky.

"Simon, I've got your things from the office. Shall I bring them round?"

"Thanks Joy, that would be good," he whispered.

"I'll come now."

Simon was clearing up when the door intercom buzzed.

Joy was holding a carrier bag. "Not much really; a couple of photos, your laptop and this." She produced Simon's Entrepreneur of the year trophy. "I sneaked them out. Your eye looks a mess. It's almost closed."

"What's happening, Joy?"

"Lucas has moved into your office. He says anyone who talks to you will be sacked. I can't stay long... You look awful. Have you seen a doctor?"

Simon sat down. "John couldn't even look me in the face. He walked straight past as I was being manhandled by Lucas' goons."

Joy went to the kitchen and put the kettle on. "He's

afraid of Lucas, afraid of what's happening."

Simon heard doors banging. "What are you doing?"

"You need something to eat." She returned with coffee and a sandwich. "There's nothing in your fridge except some cheese. I had to trim the mould off it. When did you last go shopping?"

Simon sipped the hot liquid. "Are you mothering me?"

"Simon, it's a cheese sandwich. If I was your mother you'd be eating properly and I'd be telling you, you won't find any answers in a bottle of scotch."

The dry bread stuck in Simon's mouth refusing to go anywhere. He washed it down with hot coffee. "You said John was afraid of Lucas. And you Joy, are you afraid?"

"I should be," she replied. "What you've started will end badly but you're lucky."

Simon touched his swollen eye. "Lucky. I've been thrown out of my own company and beaten up. How's that lucky."

"You don't get it do you? This is only the beginning." Joy stood up. "I've got to go. Look after yourself Simon."

The following morning Simon drove to west Wales. He needed someone to confide in, to help him clear his head and the only person he could think of was Sandra Tate. She came out of the house to meet him.

"Here," she said, handing him a rucksack. "We're going for a walk."

They set off along the lane, the clear sky reflecting blue on the waters of Cardigan Bay. Simon talked and Sandra listened as they made their way down the hill.

"This way," she pointed, leading him along a track. "We're going, past the old hill fort, down to the beach." The track narrowed to a footpath, around the base of the fort and continued along the cliff edge to a set of steps leading to a small sandy beach. At the bottom of the cliff an upturned dingy was chained to a concrete block. A man was playing leg cricket with some children. Another was fishing from rocks.

Sandra spread a blanket on the sand, sat down beside the boat and took her shoes off.

"Well," she said and pointed. "You've got the lunch."

Simon squatted and passed her the rucksack. She unpacked the food, filled two wine glasses and handed one to him. Simon sat on the upturned hull. Talking had helped. Sandra was a good listener. He felt relaxed, at peace; feelings that had become alien. The beach, holidaymakers, a picnic. It was so normal.

"What?" asked Sandra.... "You're grinning."

"I was thinking how stupid I am. Worrying about making money, wanting to save the world and tormenting myself about where I went wrong... Here I am, sat on an old boat on a lovely beach with a beautiful woman at my feet and none of it seems real. Have I been dreaming?"

Sandra sprang up. "At your feet? I don't think so." She slipped off her blouse and unbuttoned her skirt. It fell to the ground revealing a pale cream swimsuit. "Come on," she called and ran, laughing, down the beach.

Simon stripped to his underpants and chased her into the surf. He stumbled and fell landing, face first, in the freezing water.

It was late afternoon when they returned to the house. Simon showered, dressed, and joined her in the kitchen.

"Do you like sea food? I don't feel like cooking. Let's eat at the Ship Inn."

"That sounds good," said Simon.

"Great. I'll get ready and we'll go." She went upstairs.

Simon could hear water running. He felt refreshed, invigorated by the cold sea, the walk and Sandra's company. His eyes wandered along a line of photographs on the dresser; a young Sandra on a swing being pushed by a man, her father? Another of a family group taken in Paris. Simon wondered who the boy in the picture was. He picked up a silver framed photograph - a soldier in dress uniform, proud and confident, smiling. It was the same boy but older.

"That's James." Sandra was standing in the doorway, dressed in jeans and an attractive blue top.

"Your brother?"

"Yes. Dad took it at Pirbright Camp when James completed his training."

"It's a nice picture," said Simon. "Where is he now?"

Sandra took the photograph from him. "He was killed in a car crash three years ago." She placed it on the dresser and carefully positioned it.

"I'm sorry," said Simon.

Sandra picked up Simon's car keys and handed them to him. "You'll love the sea bass. They serve it with a honey and orange glaze."

A folk group was playing to a lively audience in The Ship Inn. Simon bought a bottle of wine and they stood at the end of the bar waiting for a table.

"Did you get any further, searching for your sister?"

"I haven't had time."

A young man squeezed beside them, ordered a pint of bitter and grinned. "Evening Sandra. New boyfriend?"

"Simon, this is Gareth Bridger," said Sandra. The men shook hands. "Gareth's our community policeman."

The policeman sipped his beer. "Call me Gary, please."

"Actually, Gary you might be able to help Simon. He's trying to find out about a fire at my house in the 1980s."

Gary Bridger put his drink on the bar. "1980! I wasn't even born then. Why do you want to know about a fire thirty years ago?"

"My family lived there," said Simon," My parents died in the fire. The papers said it was an arson attack. I had a sister who..."

The barman interrupted him, "Gary, some idiot has driven off the edge of the car park. The car's stuck on the beach. I think he's pissed."

The policeman drained his glass, "A policeman's lot is not a happy one and I'm not even on duty tonight." He placed the empty glass on the bar.

"You're table's ready," said the barman.

They'd finishing eating when Gary Bridger returned to the Ship Inn. A second man, older but similar in appearance was with him. The bar had emptied and the band was packing away.

"Did you get your drunken driver?" called Sandra.

"Silly sod was pissed as a fart. He's on his way to Cardigan in a police van. They'll charge him in the morning. The car's wrecked," replied the policeman. "It's just been winched off the beach." He pulled up a chair and sat down. "This is my dad. I was telling him about you Simon."

"I'm Alun," said his father. "I was one of the coppers who investigated the arson attack."

"You were at Coed Mawr?" asked Simon.

"Yes. It was a bad one." He looked at Simon. "I remember it well. We never found out who started it. Fire brigade reckoned petrol was poured through the letterbox and set alight. There were rumours... Different groups claimed responsibility. Welsh nationalists, youngsters mostly, were burning homes belonging to English holidaymakers, fighting for independence. It was nasty. The firemen had already got you and your sister out when I arrived. They tried to go back into the house but there was an almighty roar and the roof collapsed. There was no chance of rescuing your parents. It was an inferno. The heat melted the tar in the road and drove us all back... There was nothing we could do... We just stood and watched it burn."

That night Simon slept badly. He relived the fire described so vividly by Alun Bridger and woke soaked in sweat. The house was silent but he could feel Sandra's presence in the next bedroom. Seeing her on the beach, tantalising, uninhibited and full of life had aroused him. Confusing emotions competed for his attention. He hadn't lied, that afternoon, when he called Sandra beautiful. She was and he wanted her. Simon pushed back the duvet, got up and dried himself with a towel. He went to the bedroom door, opened it and listened - nothing. He hesitated, quietly shut the door, returned to bed and shut his eyes, but the demon's returned; Bridger's description of the fire haunting him. Images of the bastard James Lucas, of John Hume blanking him on the stairs appeared through the flames. Where was his sister? Was she alive? He saw his mother and father on the night of the fire, choking, trapped by the flames; the stairs and landing ablaze. Had they died in the bedroom he was in? What if there was a way of finding out who started the fire? What if Lucas could be persuaded to take him back? What if? What if? A clock downstairs struck three. 'What if's?' filled the darkness.

Muted voices woke Simon. A television was on. He checked his watch. "Damn!" It was after nine. The smell of bacon, toast and roasted coffee wafted up the stairs. Simon rinsed the taste of stale booze away and dressed quickly.

Sandra was in the kitchen by the Aga. "One egg or two? Help yourself to coffee." She pressed the remote to turn off the television as Simon poured himself a drink.

"Smells good," he said. "Two please. Thanks."

Eggs spat and crackled in the frying pan.

"How did you sleep?"

"Off and on. You know..."

"You were shouting." She slid eggs on to Simon's plate and placed it on the table. "The plate's hot."

He started to eat. "What did I say?"

She sat down. "I don't know. I heard 'Why John?' and you kept moaning 'No'. Other than that, it didn't make any sense." She got up and refilled their coffees. "What are you going to do?"

"I don't know." Simon got up and started to clear the table.

"Put them in the dishwasher."

"Where are the tablets?"

"In the cupboard on the left... You could stay here." She stared at him, waiting for a reply.

"That's very kind and I would love to stay but I've got to go back to Cambridge." Simon went upstairs and packed his things.

She was in the hall when he came down with his bag. "I'm sorry I made a fool of myself."

Simon placed his bag on the floor and put his arms around her. "No you didn't. I want to stay but there's something I must do. Sandra, you mean a great deal to me. Yesterday on the beach was fantastic. You cheered me up, broke the spell. Last night I wanted..." He kissed her on the cheek. "I'm coming back. I promise."

CHAPTER 9

Simon opened his front door and picked up an envelope. The letter was from the Home Office.

Dear Mr. Reece,

Your resignation as Managing Director of Harland Digital Limited is effective as of Thursday 29th inst. You are instructed to have no contact with employees of Harland Digital Limited either in person or electronically and reminded that all information regarding your former employer is subject to the Official Secrets Act 1989 particularly the offence of unlawful disclosure of information in six specific categories by employees and former employees of the security and intelligence services, and for current and former Crown Servants and Government contractors. Any breach or disclosure on your behalf will be a treasonable act subject to the full rigour of the law. You are also liable under the Public Records Act and any breach or disclosure will be a treasonable act subject to the full rigour of the law.

Furthermore, Director Hughes has invoked State Security Act 2019 section 58 to issue a writ of seizure and, for reasons of national security, assumed control of Harland Digital.

All Harland Digital Limited shares are now Crown property. Any shareholder claims for reimbursement will be referred to the

Board of Compensation for consideration. An application for you to complete is enclosed with this letter.

> *Yours Sincerely*
> *W. Pritchard*
> *On Behalf of the Home Secretary*

Simon poured three fingers of scotch drained the glass, refilled it and sat down. The alcohol warmed him and dulled his senses. He flicked on the television.

"Rain in the west, sunny spells later," announced the forecaster. "Mandatory DNA testing of the general public will start in two weeks."

"You'll soon be getting a letter telling you where to go," said the reporter standing outside a town hall, "And remember, there are stiff penalties if you forget."

"This morning, a car bomb was destroyed in a controlled explosion near a primary school in Southampton. An observant member of the public alerted the police who cleared the area. There were no casualties." Footage followed of terrorist suspects being dragged from their homes by OIS officers dressed in black combat gear.

"Sixty seven terrorists were detained during operation Scimitar in Manchester yesterday. It follows similar successes in London, Leeds and Cardiff."

Next came Emlyn Hughes at a press conference. "We are already seeing a reduction in violent attacks and will be going further. The Prime Minister's reinstatement of sedition as a crime gives me the tools I need to root out the cancer in our midst. We know who the people are who spew hatred and incite attacks. There will be no hiding place for them. My job is to make Britain safe..."

Reporters shouted questions, "Where are the suspects being held?" "Director Hughes, have the men been charged?" "What about..."

"My job is to make Britain safe. To deal with the threat we face and cleanse our streets. Thank you."

Simon turned off the television, poured another drink and picked up the phone.

"Deputy Director Lucas isn't available," said the receptionist.

Simon contacted lawyers asking them to fight his case, to challenge the legality of what the OIS had done. It was futile. No one dared challenge the OIS. Simon was running out of options and hope.

He phoned Sandra. "I don't know what to do."

"Simon, you've been drinking. You need to come here. To get away from Cambridge. You need to let go."

"Yes," he whispered. He cleared his throat and took a breath. "I'll come now, this minute. SOD 'EM."

"No. Simon, you're drunk. You can't drive. Get a good night's sleep and come tomorrow... Simon, did you hear what I said?... Will you do that? Promise me."

"Tomorrow... Yes," answered Simon. "I promise I'll come tomorrow. Sandra... I'm sorry."

"Don't be stupid. Just get here safely."

An alarm woke Simon early. Hot water purged the alcohol induced throb in his head as he pieced together the conversation with Sandra. He'd apologised, that much he could remember, but why? Had he said something unpleasant?

There was a knock. Simon pulled on a dressing gown and answered the door.

The postman held out a letter. "Recorded delivery. You have a date with the OIS. Everyone's getting one."

Simon ripped the envelope open.

Dear Mr. Reece,

You are ordered to report to the Guildhall in Market Square at 10am on the 16th of July for an identity check, DNA testing and fitting of your microchip. You are required to bring two forms of identification with you. NOTE - Failure to attend for micro-chipping is a criminal offence punishable by a one thousand pound fine and or six months in prison.

Simon rang Sandra to apologise again and explain he would be staying in Cambridge for a couple more days.

The Guildhall was crowded. Sullen people, corralled behind barriers, waited. A little girl whimpered. They shuffled towards a curtained area at the front of the hall.

"Photographic I.D. and your letter." demanded a uniformed woman. Simon handed her his papers.

She scanned the passport. "Put your chin on the rest." She photographed Simon's left eye then the right. A printer ejected a label. The woman stuck the label to a sterile specimen bag and handed it to Simon. "It's a serious offence to tamper with this label or to remove it." She pointed to a black canvas cubicle, and returned the identity documents. "In there!"

Simon went through to the cubicle. A policeman was sitting at a desk with an electronic finger print machine in front of him.

"Press the four fingers of your left hand on the screen," he ordered. Simon obeyed. "Now the thumb." He did the same with the right hand, grunted and pointed. "Through there."

The next cubicle was lined with plastic sheeting. Plastic had been spread on the floor and used to make a ceiling.

An orderly dressed in white, wearing gloves, a plastic cap and a face-mask nodded to him."Have you eaten anything in the last two hours?" The orderly asked and sniffed loudly.

"No," replied Simon.

Have you smoked in the last two hours?"

"I don't smoke."

"Have you chewed gum in the last two hours?" He sniffed again.

"No."

"How long ago did you last clean your teeth?"

"This morning, about three hours ago," answered Simon.

"Good. Rinse your mouth." The orderly handed Simon a plastic cup half filled with water. "You can either swallow it or spit it there." He nodded to a plastic bucket. Simon swallowed.

The orderly took the specimen kit from Simon, opened it, removed a sample tube and microchip. He opened the tube and removed a swab stick. "I need you to keep your mouth wide open for 60 seconds." The orderly worked the swab around Simon's gums and the inside of his cheeks. He placed the swab in the tube, clipped the outer lid into place, pulled the stick out and sealed the tube leaving the sterile swab inside.

"Almost done." The orderly pulled his mask to one side and blew his nose. "Are you right or left handed?"

"Left handed."

"Roll up your right sleeve and lift up your arm."

The orderly rubbed his arm with surgical spirit and loaded the injector. He felt for a soft spot, pinched the skin and pressed the plunger home.

"Shit. That bloody hurt," said Simon.

"Yes, I'm sorry. Nearly done." The orderly held a scanner over the imbedded microchip. There was a beep. A number, Simon's identifier, appeared on the screen.

"That's it," said the orderly. "NEXT."

Simon was walking home when Sandra rang.

"How did it go?"

"A spotty kid with flu poked about in my mouth." He stopped at a pedestrian crossing.

"I got my letter yesterday, telling me when to have my implant. I'm going on Thursday," replied Sandra. "Have you done anything about finding your sister?"

The green man started to flash. "I've not had time." Simon stepped aside to avoid a woman pushing a supermarket trolley straight at him. "Excuse me!"

"Get stuffed," snapped the woman.

"Excuse you?" asked Sandra. "What for?"

"Not you. It was a woman on the crossing. She nearly ran me down with a shopping trolley."

"Oh!.. Simon, why don't you write to the chief constable of Dyfed Powys police and ask if they'll reopen the case?"

"What for?"

"Don't you see? With the new database they might be able to find her. She's your twin - the DNA. There would be a match."

"After nearly forty years! They wouldn't be interested," replied Simon.

"Can you think of another way?"

That afternoon Simon wrote the letter and took it to the Post Office. A plump woman in her fifties was seated behind the counter. She greeted him with a broad smile. "Hello Simon. How can I help you today?"

"How did you know my name?"

She pointed to her computer. "It's fantastic. Tells me everyone's name." She turned the machine so he could see. There, on the screen, were his details; a photograph, his name and address. Simon felt under his arm. It was tender and starting to bruise.

"There's a scanner in the counter." She pointed. "Clever isn't it? Identifies everyone." She took the letter. "First or second class?"

Emlyn Hughes highlighted a row of figures, put the report down and looked out of his office window. London was basking in sunshine. A blue sky pierced, in the distance, by the Shard. Near it, a small dot, a passenger aircraft turning, on its approach to City Airport. He returned to the report and smiled. His plan was working. Five thousand arrests and terror attacks down by twenty four percent but there was more work to do. Thousands more suspects had been identified and thousands more, illegal immigrants and runners dodging micro-chipping, still to be tracked down.

"The Prime Minister's car has arrived," said an aide.

Hughes hurried down to the underground car park, greeted Max Roberts and showed him around the new OIS headquarters. The tour had been well rehearsed. At each department, a team leader would explain its purpose.

"Interesting," said the Prime Minister in the first department. In the second he cut the explanation short. Hughes took the PM to control room seven, a dark cavernous office filled with computer workstations. The room was silent, no telephones rang, no noise, except the quiet hum of air conditioning cooling lines of soundless, headphone wearing watchers.

"This is where we monitor watch list targets. You'll find this interesting," explained Director Hughes. He put his hand on an operative's shoulder. "Williams, tell the Prime Minister how it works."

Williams removed his headset. "Regis' PCL uses mobile phone network location augmented by sensors at major intersections - railway stations, banks, public buildings and other places to follow the movements of watch list targets."

"What's PCL?" interrupted the Prime Minister.

"I'm sorry. It's Personal Chip Locator," explained Williams. "At the moment my workstation," he pointed at the screens in front of him, "is tracking twelve hundred targets." He waited for some encouragement, some interest but the Prime Minister was looking at his watch.

The computer buzzed. A small window opened containing a picture of a face. Williams expanded it. "The alarm went off because of this target," He leant forward to read the details. "Ahmed Hafiz has entered a level two security area."

The Prime Minister bent down to have a look. "Who?"

The operator touched a key and opened Hafiz's file on the screen. "He's a petty thief, two convictions for burglary, one for assault and he's just returned from a holiday in Turkey." He pointed to a box. "Here Prime Minister, can you see? There's a flag on his bank account because of an unusual transaction. Someone paid six thousand pounds cash into it last week."

Max Roberts reached for a chair and sat down beside Williams. "Regis can tell you all this at the push of a button."

"It can do more than that Prime Minister," said Hughes. "Tell the Prime Minister where the money came from?"

Williams opened another window. "It was paid into Hafiz's bank account in the Halifax branch. Regis also tracks CCTV facial recognition for known targets. It automatically identified the payee as Masood Khan, a known recruiter. We're still looking for Khan."

"Tell the Prime Minister where Hafiz is," said Hughes.

Williams opened a map and pointed to a flashing red marker. "There Prime Minister, can you see." Roberts nodded. "Hafiz has just left Trafalgar Square and is on Whitehall, walking towards Downing Street."

The operator typed a message, pressed send and switched to a matrix of CCTV images of Whitehall. He selected a camera and used a joystick to zoom in on a solitary figure walking slowly along the pavement. The man was holding a guide-book and eating an ice cream.

"It shouldn't take long," said Williams.

Intrigued by the unfolding drama the Prime Minister sat and waited. The man approached a couple and handed them his phone. They watched as Hafiz posed beside the Cenotaph and the woman took his picture.

A black van approached at speed. It stopped. Three masked men jumped out. They pushed the couple aside and seized Hafiz. Ice cream splattered across the road. He struggled as they handcuffed him. The woman was shouting and gesturing.

"She's getting very excited," said the Prime Minister. "It's a shame there's no sound."

The men scanned Hafiz's arm, hooded him and bundled him into the van. It sped away leaving the confused couple on the pavement.

"Excellent work," said the Prime Minister. "Emlyn, is there somewhere we can have a private chat?"

Hughes took the Prime Minister up to his office and shut the door. Cold meats and salads had been laid out for them. They sat at the table by the window and talked about old times.

"Do you remember the drugs raid in Tregaron when I tipped you off?" asked Emlyn.

"Remember it! I lost a barn full of cannabis, all my dealers and a bloody fortune."

"But they never caught you." Emlyn Hughes sat back in his chair. "Have you ever wondered why I warned you?"

Roberts stuffed a cherry tomato into his mouth. "Because, Emlyn, you're a greedy bugger. You knew I'd pay."

"That wasn't the reason. The money was nice but I wanted the leader of the Free Wales Army and I knew you could give me the evidence to nail him."

"So you're a hero. You got your inspector's pips and a medal with that arrest." Roberts pushed his plate away and stared at Hughes. "You still owe me for that and you owe me for this." He waved his arm around the office. "Director of Internal Security. You've done well for yourself Emlyn. Not bad for a provincial policemen."

"What is it Max? What do you want?"

"Emily Sharp is becoming a problem," said the Prime Minister. "I've spoken to her but she won't keep her mouth shut. The stupid bitch has been complaining again. Moaning about human rights. She was on Question Time last night calling the OIS 'Nazis' and the mass arrests a disgrace."

"I saw it," said Hughes.

"The audience cheered her and clapped."

"I agree, she's a trouble maker," replied Hughes. "Max,

you pissed her off when you gave her Culture Media and Sport. She wanted Defence."

"Defence! She's not fit to be minister of curtains and fluffy cushions. I made the bloody woman a minister in my cabinet - and this is how she repays me." Roberts' cheeks were flushed. "I won't have disloyalty in the ranks. It's not the first time she's opened her big mouth and stirred things up. You have to deal with her."

Emlyn Hughes nodded.

"Good." Roberts looked at his watch. "Must get on."

The OIS Director accompanied Roberts down to the basement car park. They stepped out of the lift.

"The performance with that character on Whitehall," said Roberts. "Was it really necessary?"

Hughes waited until the motorcade had gone.

Back in his office he sent for Williams. "Hafiz, it was a genuine arrest, you didn't stage it?"

"No Sir," replied Williams.

"Good. The Prime Minister was impressed. Well done... "Where's Hafiz now?"

"He's being interrogated."

"Excellent," said Director Hughes. "You may go."

Ahmed Hafiz was manacled to a chair in the basement of the OIS building.

"I'll ask you again," shouted his interrogator. "Where is Masood Khan?"

"I told you. I don't know."

"What was the six thousand pounds for?"

A man standing behind Hafiz held a pistol to the prisoner's temple and cocked the weapon.

"Think very carefully before you answer. This room is soundproof. No one will hear you die. The six thousand pounds. We know he paid it into your bank account. Why?"

"He was repaying me. I loaned him money to buy a car."

"You're a liar." The gun discharged shattering Hafiz's eardrum. He screamed.

"The next bullet will be in your brain. WHERE IS KHAN?"

Hafiz whimpered and bowed his head.

"We're wasting our time. He doesn't know," said the interrogator. "Send him to High Lingham Detention Camp."

A silent alarm triggered in the security office at Leeds railway station. Someone without a microchip had walked up the stairs at the back of the station. A camera panned to the stairwell leading into the station's atrium. A facial recognition programme scanned the area. In seconds hundreds of faces were checked against Regis and identified. A screen in the security office locked on one face; a young man. Beneath the face, a red bar, highlighting a name, flashed across the bottom of the screen. "WANTED - Masood Khan."

The duty sergeant shouted to his colleagues in their rest room. The men grabbed their weapons.

"The target is called Khan." The sergeant pointed at the screen. "He's a white male on the south side of the concourse. You can't miss him. He's wearing a grey thaub and carrying a blue rucksack."

"A grey what?" shouted one of his men.

"A fuckin shirt to his ankles, you pillock," yelled the sergeant, "Now get after him."

Khan saw the armed officers running along the platform. A train pulled into the station blocking his view.

"Get out of the way. MOVE," shouted the policemen, barging their way through the crowd.

Khan turned, hurried down the stairs and vanished into the street.

CHAPTER 10

The chief constable of Dyfed Powys Police didn't read Simon Reece's letter. Instead, the letter was passed to a liaison officer to deal with. She replied explaining that all unsolved cases remain open but unless new evidence comes to light the police authority are unable to take any further action. Her reply went on to say, the secondment of constabulary resources to the OIS made investigating old cases extremely difficult. Priorities had to be made and while the Chief Constable understood Mr. Reece's concern, and offered his condolences, he was unable to help regarding the fire that killed Mr. Reece's parents.

"What do you think?" said Simon and handed the letter to Sandra.

She read it again. "Not even a mention of your sister... Doesn't leave you much, does it? What are you going to do now?"

"About the fire! What can I do?" He poured Sandra another drink and joined her on the sofa. "I do have some good news. The sale of my step-parent's house was completed yesterday. The money's in the bank. I'm solvent again and," he smiled, "I've found a lawyer who is prepared to fight my claim for compensation for Harland."

"How much is the company worth?"

Simon shook his head. "If you'd asked me six months ago I would have said eight million. Now the government is using Regis it's probably worth ten times that but they won't pay it."

"What do you mean? Surely they've got to pay what it's worth."

Simon put his arm around Sandra. "What's anything worth! The value of something is what someone is willing to pay - nothing more... And the government won't be grateful buyers, willing to pay a fair price. They'll screw me."

The fire spat a piece of bark onto the rug. Sandra jumped up, grabbed the tongs and tossed the smouldering ember back into the grate. "Damn! It's made a hole."

"I'll buy you a new rug."

She sat down again and snuggled in. "It's old. Don't bother." She looked up at him. You mustn't give up, ever."

"Kilburn Plumbing Services," said the sign on the side of the van. It drove slowly along Ashworth Road and pulled onto the pavement outside a mock Tudor house. A light drizzle was falling. An old lady, wearing a plastic rain hat, squeezed past the van. She bent down, picked up a little dog, stepped over a puddle and scowled at the driver. The driver, a tall man in white overalls, smiled at her. He got out and walked to the corner of the road.

A small blue Renault car turned into Ashworth Road and slowed. A woman was driving. Beside her sat a man and behind them two young children. The Renault pulled around the front of the van onto a hard standing in front of the house.

The man got out, opened a rear door and unfastened his daughter's seatbelt. His wife stood at the back of the car. She waved to the lady with the dog and began to unload shopping.

The man in white overalls put his hand in his pocket,

pressed a button on his mobile phone and walked casually along Elgin Avenue, towards Maida Vale underground station. A black estate car with darkened windows pulled alongside him and stopped. The man got in and was driven away.

A telephone rang on Hughes' desk. His secretary answered. "Another terrorist attack, Sir. A government minister - Mrs. Sharp and her family blown up outside their north London home. There are no survivors."

Emlyn Hughes nodded, walked back to the desk and took the phone. "A huge bomb you say, in a van. Have you told the PM? Good. Yes, and the children so young. I agree, it's dreadful news." He handed the receiver to the secretary and dictated a statement that the killers of the Sharp family would be brought to justice. "The OIS," he declared, "would find and punish the perpetrators."

Early on Sunday morning Simon walked down to the village. Llangranog beach was deserted and the car park empty. The owner of the general store was setting up for the day, hanging buckets, spades, inflatables and beach chairs on the wall. He secured a postcard rack to the doorpost and went inside. Simon followed and came out with a bottle of milk and a newspaper. He stood and read the headline. "Killer Khan named." A picture of Masood Khan filled the front page. "The OIS have named Victor Swain also known as Masood Khan as the main suspect in the bombing of Emily Sharp. Khan, a known jihadist, was identified from CCTV images as he made his escape through Maida Vale underground station..."

A police car cruised past. It stopped and reversed back. The passenger window wound down.

"Morning Simon," said the driver. "You're out early."

Simon bent down to look into the car. "Hello Gary. I didn't realise it was you. We needed some milk." He pointed to the bottle.

Gary Bridger nodded. "I saw your car outside Sandra's.

Get in. I'll give you a lift back."

"This is a nasty business," said Simon pointing to the paper.

"Yeah. Khan won't get far. Hatchet Hughes will get him," said Gary. "You can be sure of that. Do you know he was my dad's sergeant?"

" Who's Hatchet Hughes?" asked Simon.

"Hughes, the OIS Director. Dad calls him Hatchet. Hates him. Said he was an evil sod and bent, happy to frame anyone. He says, 'Everyone knew it.' He made chief constable before I joined the force."

The car turned into the lane leading to Coed Mawr.

"Hatchet Hughes," repeated Simon. "I met him once. He certainly did a hatchet job on me."

Gary Bridger stopped the car. "What do you mean?"

Simon told Gary how the OIS had sacked him and stolen Harland Digital. "Right now a sly, scheming bastard named Lucas, is sitting behind my desk, running my company."

Gary Bridger's police radio crackled into life. "Gary, your bacon roll's getting cold."

The policemen laughed. "You see how tough it is crime fighting on the thin blue line." He spoke into the radio. "Stick it in the microwave. I'm on my way."

Simon got out of the car. "I'll walk. Thanks for the lift."

"You should talk to my dad about Hughes," suggested Gary Bridger and drove away.

Simon walked back to the house and told Sandra about his conversation with Gary.

"Talk to his dad," she said.

"I'm not interested in Alun Bridger's stories about Hughes."

"Why not?" said Sandra. "He might know where your sister was taken."

CHAPTER 11

James Lucas watched the CCTV footage again. A fleeting shot of Masood Khan turning and running through Maida Vale underground station. There was something familiar about the man, the blue rucksack, the way he turned and ran. He looked at the email the video had come with. It was from Frank Wilbourn, Head of Communications and had been sent to Director Hughes and himself. Lucas had seen the clip before, on the evening news. It was key evidence, the bulletin had said, identifying Khan as the bomber, the Sharp family's killer.

Lucas pulled up Masood Khan's file on his computer and opened Khan's video archive. The bank recording of Khan paying six thousand pounds into Hafiz's account was in the folder. So was the video he'd watched from Maida Vale? If it was, where was the other video, the one from Leeds station?

Someone had removed it. Lucas tapped his finger on his lip. Had Khan ever been to Maida Vale?

He picked up the phone and rang Hughes' private line. There was no answer. Lucas wasn't surprised. Since his move to Harland Digital Hughes had grown distant. Lucas felt sidelined. Hughes rarely discussed operational matters with him anymore and the deputy director resented being sidelined. Lucas was bored with the technical aspects of Regis. The database was the OIS's most powerful tool. He was in sole charge of it and yet, removed from the centre of things he was becoming and outsider, a forgotten bystander.

Lucas summoned Harland's technical director, to his office. "John how frequently does Regis backup itself?"

"Regis has two mirror copies which update continuously. The software backs up to storage every six hours. The backup files are indexed and stored for three weeks. Monthly backups are also kept."

"If someone removed a video, from a target's file could you recover it?"

"Easily. If a video has been deleted it will still be in the backup copies," replied Hume, "and the audit log would tell us when it was removed. It should also tell us who's responsible. Even if the audit log has been tampered with, and that would need high level administrator access, the backup will show which six hour period it was taken in."

"Good. A video file has been removed. I want it found and I want to know who took it. I'll send you the details and John, this is confidential. I don't want anyone else to know. Do you understand?"

Simon was sitting at the bar of The Ship Inn when Alun and Gary Bridger arrived. He bought them drinks and they moved to a table where they could talk.

Alun swallowed a mouthful of beer. "So you want to know about Hatchet Hughes." He put his glass on the table. "He was my sergeant."

"Yes. Gary told me."

"I was a probationer when your house was torched. Hughes was in charge. He wasn't interested in investigating the fire. I didn't understand why but he just went through the motions."

"Why would he do that?" asked Simon.

The retired policemen took another drink and wiped his mouth. "I don't know but I can tell you one thing; he was bent. A backhander to look the other way, fabricating evidence. You didn't get on the wrong side of him."

"You should have said something. Reported him."

Alun Hughes snorted. "I was a kid. I thought he was a brilliant copper. He caught criminals, got results. It was only later I realised how evil he was... By then it was too late."

Gary Bridger stood up. "Do you want another drink Dad, Simon?"

Simon drained his glass and passed it to Gary. "Alun, you said, 'It was too late'. What do you mean by that?"

"I wanted to buy a car. Nothing flash. Hughes offered to lend me money. He gave me a cheque for three hundred pounds. The strange thing was, the cheque wasn't in his name. Like a fool I banked it. Later, when I repaid him, he gave me back a hundred pounds in cash and told me to keep it. 'It's your share,' he said, 'A little thank you for helping a friend of mine out of a spot of trouble.'"

Gary returned with the drinks and sat down.

"Whose name was the cheque in?" asked Simon.

"I can't remember. It didn't seem important but, you see don't you? He'd used me to launder a bribe. After that what could I say? I had no proof he'd given me the cheque. He knew exactly what he was doing. He set me up and I wasn't the only one. Hughes was like a poison. He used everyone around him - controlling, bullying."

Sandra joined them. Gary pulled up an extra chair.

"Thanks Gary." Sandra sat down. "So, has Alun been able to help?"

"The thing is Alun," said Simon, "I, that is Sandra and I, were wondering if there was anything from the fire that might help."

"You mean identify the arsonist?"

"No. I was thinking of my sister Pamela. I want to find her. Do you know where she went?"

Alun shook his head. "Can't help you. It was chaos. The babies were taken away in an ambulance. That's the last I saw of them. I remember it driving away. I'd just picked up the coat."

"Coat, what coat?" asked Sandra.

"There was a man's coat - a donkey jacket. It was hanging in the hedge. The coat was scorched. I thought it was evidence and showed it to Hughes. He bagged it and put it on the back seat of his police car. Knowing Hughes, he probably threw it away."

"He was a copper. Why would he do that? asked Gary.

His father shrugged.

"It was forty years ago," said Simon. "The jacket, coat, whatever it was, will be long gone."

"He might have kept it as some kind of insurance," suggested Sandra. "To keep a hold over whoever set the fire, maybe even to blackmail them."

"You mean he knew who did it?" said Simon.

"Maybe."

"So what? None of this helps me find Pamela."

Sandra took Simon's hand. "What if it led to the murderer of your parents? Wouldn't you want to know?"

"Yes of course I would," said Simon. "But how?"

"If it was the killer's coat his DNA might be on it."

"This is all speculation," said Simon. "A coat that might or might not exist. DNA that can't have survived and an arsonist who, after forty years, is dead for all we know."

A bell rang behind the bar. "Last orders," shouted the landlord.

Officer Phillips was bored. It was late afternoon and nearly the end of his shift. He parked on Headingley Road, his automatic number plate recognition camera scanning vehicles heading towards Leeds. The ANPR triggered. An untaxed van was driving past. Phillips ignored it. A pedestrian crossing, behind the policeman's car, stopped the traffic and a group of schoolgirls crossed the road, followed by a white man dressed in a Muslim thaub. Phillips sat in the unmarked car and watched, in his mirror, as the girls and the man approached. He switched on his mobile scanner and waited. There were a series of beeps as the schoolgirls passed. The scanner was logging their details and storing them to memory. Then, the man drew level with the car. The scanner didn't respond. There was no signal, no identity details appeared on the display. The man wasn't micro chipped.

Phillips jumped from the car, "Stay where you are."

The man ran, barging the girls aside, scattering them into the road. There was a scream. A vehicle swerved. The man glanced back. A passerby stuck his leg out tripping the escaping fugitive. He stumbled and landed in a heap. The policeman wrenched his arms back and handcuffed them.

A crowd gathered around the kneeling policeman as he radioed for help. Officer Phillips had arrested Masood Khan the man wanted for the London bombing.

That evening the OIS collected Khan from Leeds, hooded the prisoner and drove him to London.

Khan stumbled as he was manhandled down seemingly endless stairs. Heavy footsteps echoed on a stone floor. The hood was removed. Khan squinted in the glare of fluorescent lights. He was standing beside a table in a corridor with dirty yellow painted brick walls and a low vaulted ceiling.

A guard unfastened his handcuffs. "Strip."

Khan rubbed his wrists and tried to focus.

"I won't tell you again. Get undressed."

Khan pulled the thaub over his head and stood up.

A muffled scream echoed along the corridor.

"And the pants and socks."

Khan stripped naked, covering his privates with his hands.

Guards marched him to a cell. Rough hands pushed him in.

The door slammed shut.

Khan stood still in the icy, dimly lit cell. It was empty except for a concrete bed against the wall, a metal toilet and a sink. He started to shake. A red boiler suit was lying on the bed. The cloth smelt of disinfectant and scratched as he pulled it on. It was huge. His feet didn't reach the end of the legs. There were no buttons or belt. The suit hung open, its coarse material chafing his skin, offering no warmth, no comfort. He sat on the concrete platform, curled into a ball and shut his eyes.

He didn't know what time it was when the guards came. They took Khan to a small room containing a metal table and three canvas chairs, and shackled him to the table. He was alone. A strip light cracked and flickered, unable to illuminate properly. White tiles, cracked and smeared with decades of grime, covered the walls. He tried to move but the table legs were bolted to the floor. Cold passed, from the stone floor, through Khan's bare feet and up his legs. They cramped. He lifted one foot and then the other to ease the pain.

The door opened. Two men entered. The first big, thirtyish, dressed in a grey suit and with a military bearing, tough looking. They sat down opposite Khan. The second man was older, in his sixties. His hair, like his suit, was black, thinning and greasy. He opened a packet of cigarettes, lit one, opened a folder and studied it. A guard entered carrying a tray of coffee, and cups.

"Ashtray," barked the older man. He looked at Khan. "Victor Swain! You must be thirsty." He poured coffee and pushed it across the table. Unable to raise his hands, Khan bent down, gripped the cup with both hands and drank greedily. The hot coffee burnt his mouth.

The guard returned. "I'm sorry Sir. We don't have any." He placed a saucer on the table.

"Why Khan?" asked the older man. "Why change your name to Khan?"

Khan didn't reply.

"You're Victor Swain, twenty-six, a small time thug from Huddersfield."

"My name is Masood Khan. I've done nothing. Why am I here?"

The older man inhaled and flicked ash into the saucer. "With a liking for violence." He coughed smoke and spittle across the table. "It says here you robbed an old woman and broke her arm."

"That was eleven years ago. I was fifteen. I paid for it." Khan leaned forward. "Three years I did. You learn a lot in prison. I grew up there. Became a man."

"You converted to Islam and changed your name. Tell me why."

Khan looked at his questioner. "Khan... It means leader." He smiled, a cocky self-assured sneer of a smile. "I saw the light. Mohammed spoke to me and soon I'll be a free man Inshallah."

"God willing you say. Did Mohammed tell you to blow up the Sharp family. Murder two little children."

"It wasn't me. I didn't do it," replied Khan confidently. It's forbidden."

"We have a video which shows you running away after you triggered the bomb."

Khan shrugged. "Allahu A'lam."

"What does that mean? English! Speak to me in bloody English..." The older man convulsed, overwhelmed by a coughing fit, his face red.

Khan waited for him to stop. "Allah knows the truth."

"Does he? I'm not asking Allah. I'm asking you... Ahmed Hafiz. Tell me about him."

"Ahmed, what about him?"

"Ahmed Hafiz, has confessed. Says he was the bomb maker." The older man studied Khan watching for a response. "What was the six thousand pounds for? Was it to pay for the van you used, the van that Hafiz bought?"

The older man shoved a photograph across the table.

"LOOK AT IT."

Khan studied the picture. It was a still from a surveillance video showing a man running along a platform. Behind him a sign, *Maida Vale*. The man in the picture looked exactly like him. "That isn't me." He looked at the younger man. "I've never been to Maida Vale in my life. I swear it on the Holy Koran... Please, you must believe me."

The older man banged the table, startling Khan. "Who else is working with you?" He nodded to his colleague.

The younger man stood up, removed his jacket and carefully placed it on the back of his chair.

"We have plenty of time... You will tell us everything," said the older man and lit another cigarette.

CHAPTER 12

Leaning forward, Emlyn Hughes could see skyscrapers rising through the haze. A wisp of steam drifted lazily from the top of one. The executive jet banked and his first view of Houston vanished from sight. The plane lost height as it turned. Rays of sunshine made an arc through the cabin. A different landscape appeared. The plane was lower now, travelling faster it seemed, over housing estates and shopping malls. A truck was tipping garbage in a landfill. A busy road appeared and quickly vanished.

"We're about to land at George Bush airport," said the cabin attendant and took her seat. They passed the airfield's perimeter fence. Hughes tensed, anticipating the moment the plane would touch the ground. It was always the same. Hughes enjoyed flying but not landing. He shut his eyes and felt the bump as the plane hit the runway. It taxied to a private standing where a large black sedan and two people carriers were waiting.

C.J. Hunt, Systron Security's CEO welcomed Hughes and his deputy Lucas as they stepped down from the plane. "Welcome to Texas. This is Ted Shuber. Ted's Deputy Under Secretary of Homeland Security, in charge of technology."

A minder guided them to the waiting car. Suited bodyguards, big men with dark glasses, boarded the people carriers.

They exchanged pleasantries as the motorcade sped south on Interstate 69.

"Your office has booked a suite at the Sheraton," said C.J. "There's a good Mexican restaurant near there, the Caracol. I've reserved a private room for tomorrow tonight. You'll like it."

The motorcade turned west onto North Loop Freeway pushing its way through the traffic, with flashing lights and sirens.

"How are your preparations for Regis coming along?" asked the OIS director casually.

"Pretty damn good," replied C.J. "Nico tells me her trials with Homeland Security have been a great success. It's a superb bit of software. Isn't that right Ted?"

"We're ready to go live as soon as the President says so."

"Nico! Who's Nico?" asked Hughes.

"Nicola Synful," explained Lucas. "She's Systron's head of programming."

Hughes nodded.

"There is one snag though," said Shuber. "We won't be able to use the microchip module. Not officially. The senate won't go for it. The President wants it in so what we propose is to install the whole package and bring in the micro-chipping gradually. Start with paroled felons, drug users, individuals where no one will object. We can chip the rest of the population later."

"Create some fear," suggested Hughes. "Some terrorist bombs and high profile shootings and the senate will soon fall into line."

Shuber smiled. "Is that how you did it, persuaded Joe Shmo to do as he was told? A stunt like that might work in England but not here. No Sir. Your average American would be sat on their porch with a ten gauge and no intention of being chipped by the state. We've a long tradition of distrust."

The following day Hughes and Lucas were driven, downtown to Homeland Security's Houston office on the corner of Bell Street and Travis. A meeting room had been prepared on the 23rd floor and technical staff from both Systron and Homeland Security were on hand to field questions. Losing interest, Emlyn Hughes became distracted, glancing out of the window, leaving Lucas to follow the conversation, something he struggled to do.

Lucas, out of his depth with the Americans, realised he should have brought John Hume with him and said very little but there was one issue he knew he had to raise. "I know we've discussed sharing information but can you confirm the UK will have unrestricted access to American Regis data?"

Shuber answered. "That's a question that's still under consideration. In practical terms there's no issue. The problem is we aren't allowed to share information on American citizens with foreign powers. You see..."

"That unfair," interrupted Hughes. "When we've offered to let you have unrestricted access to our database."

Shuber shrugged. "Maybe, but we will share everything we have on people who aren't US citizens. That's the official line."

"So you'll understand if we do the same," snapped Hughes.

The under secretary toyed with his pen for a moment. "If you shut the door on us it would be a big mistake." He leant forward. "Off the record, well - let's say we'll find a way to bend the rules a bit."

When the meeting was over they moved across town to the Caracol Restaurant where a private room had been booked.

C.J. ordered tequila shots. "You like tequila?"

"Never tasted it," said Hughes.

"Hell. Never tasted tequila. OK. Here's how you drink it. Lick your thumb and forefinger and sprinkle salt on them like this... Hold the glass and lime in your other hand. Good. Now lick the salt, down the shot in one and suck on the lime wedge. Ready..." He sank his drink. "That's the way. You got it. Hey, we're celebrating let's have another."

Later C.J. took Hughes to one side. "Our private arrangement. It's all set up like we said. I can show you how it works before you fly back."

Hughes returned to the office block on Bell Street and Travis the following day. It was early and he came alone. He stopped the taxi a block away and walked, hurrying along the sunless, windswept boulevard to keep his appointment. The skyscraper loomed above him, a glass tower reaching into the stratosphere. This time there was no VIP welcome, no plush meeting room on the 23rd floor, no fawning secretaries or beefy security men. The night guard behind the reception desk was ignoring the monitors. He looked vacant, asleep, a somnambulist, unaware and uncaring. A coffee stained newspaper lit by a small lamp lay, discarded, on the desk.

C.J. Hunt was waiting behind a column on the far side of the atrium, furtive, silent. He pointed at the camera. Ignoring the lift, the two men climbed the back stairs. Fluorescent lights showing every ugly crack. Broken treads and flaking paint shaming the grand façade of the Homeland Security building. Hughes' laboured breathing, punctuated by their heavy footsteps, echoing on each flight. C.J. stopped on a landing and waited for Hughes to catch up. He pointed to a small, dimly lit office. They didn't speak until the door was closed. A laptop was open on the desk. It's display flickered into life as Hughes typed. A picture appeared on the screen; a tropical blue sea, sand, palm trees and a luxury yacht anchored in the bay. A new window opened; 'Cayman National Bank.' C.J. Hunt grinned and unfolded a small piece of paper. Hughes read the numbers and typed, faster now, impatient to see. An account opened.

"There," said C.J. "Two million Dollars. I didn't lie and it's all yours. Tell Max Roberts, thanks," said C.J. "It's a sweet deal. Uncle Sam is paying Systron top dollar for Regis."

"And the rest?"

"Relax Emlyn. Hell. I haven't forgotten. The licensing fee, two hundred thousand a month, we said, will be paid into the same account."

Lucas had checked out and was waiting in the lobby when Hughes got back to the hotel.

"Good morning Director." He looked at his watch. "The plane leaves at twelve."

"I needed some air," said Hughes. "Went for a walk." Hughes hardly spoke as they were driven to the airport. Lucas' attempts at conversation went unanswered. He gave up trying to engage with his boss and the two men sat in awkward silence.

The car stopped at the airport steps.

"I'm surprised C.J. didn't come to see us off," said Lucas.

"What for? We've done our business... He'll still be sleeping off the booze he sank."

A steward showed them aboard and handed them menus. "We'll being serving dinner after takeoff. Would you like a aperitif."

"Champagne," said Hughes. "Bring a bottle."

"And you Sir?"

"Just water. No. A soda... Do you have a Sprite?" Lucas opened the ventilator above his head and took a deep breath.

The steward nodded.

They were airborne when the steward came to ask what

they would like to eat.

"I'll have the fish," said Hughes, "with a green salad."

Lucas handed his menu to the steward. "I'm not hungry."

Hughes ate his meal covered his eyes and slept. Lucas listened to his boss' gentle snoring and wondered where he went when he stepped out for some air.

Gary Bridger sounded excited when he phoned Simon and said he'd found something. They met at the cliff top viewing point overlooking Llangranog Beach. The policeman was sitting in his car as Simon arrived. Simon joined him. A gust of wind caught the door slamming it against his leg.

"Careful! It's always windy up here," said Gary. They watched white horses crashing against the cliff. A lone kite surfer bounced across the waves. The surfer took off, cleared a big wave and disappeared behind it, emerging moments later. "I was thinking what my dad said about a coat so I got a friend in records to search the evidence log. He found nothing in the computer files but later he gave me this."

Gary produced a sheet of paper and handed it to Simon. "It's a photocopy of a page from the 1980 evidence ledger. Everything was on paper those days." Gary pointed to an entry. "Right under our noses. The coat, the one dad found. According to this it was in the evidence storage warehouse at Carmarthen."

Simon read the hand written record. "Exhibit number EH7 Burnt miner's type donkey jacket recovered from scene of fatal arson attack at Coed Mawr, Pontgarreg 15th September 1980 Location bay 67 shelf 24."

"EH7 what does that mean?" asked Simon.

"Emlyn Hughes exhibit number seven. It refers to a statement that Hughes would have made at the time. So dad was right. There was a coat and Hughes booked it into the evidence store."

"Can we get hold of it?" asked Simon. "Will it still be there after all these years?"

Gary shook his head. "The coat should still be there but it's a secure area with limited access. And even if you got the coat, any DNA evidence would be compromised. It would be useless."

A blast of wind shook the car. Rain splattered the windscreen obscuring the view.

"Then we must get the case re-examined," said Simon. "But how? The chief constable's letter said they would not look at it without new evidence and the coat isn't new evidence."

CHAPTER 13

Simon looked up at the shabby sign 'Plaid Cymru Advice Centre.' The shop looked dilapidated; flaking green paint and dirty windows. 'Aaron Green - Assembly Member South West Wales,' said the paper stuck to the window. A limp net curtain shielded the inside from view. Simon opened the door and went in. A young woman wedged behind a small desk was on the phone. She gestured to a chair piled with election posters. Simon moved the posters and sat down. It had been Sandra's idea to contact Aaron Green and, sitting in the cramped office, Simon was already regretting it.

"He's a campaigner," she'd said. "If anyone can get the case reopened he can."

"Diolch," said the woman, "Hwyl." She replaced the receiver. "You Mr. Reece? That was Aaron on the phone. He's in the car, on the way back from Cardiff and will be about ten minutes. Would you like a coffee while you wait?" She boiled a kettle, perched on a wobbly table, handed Simon a mug of brown sludge and told him her life story.

The door opened. "Mr. Reece? Aaron Green. Sorry I'm late; committee meeting. Couldn't get away." The assembly member was wearing a tailored business suit. He looked overweight but radiated energy.

Simon followed Green through to another office, a well ordered inner sanctum. The desk clear except for a laptop and a phone. A framed cartoon of the Max Roberts in a fascist uniform hung on a wall. Someone had added a moustache using a red felt pen. Simon smiled.

"Childish humour. It helps," said Green and shrugged. "My secretary said something about a police matter where you need help."

Simon explained the circumstances of his parent's death and why he'd come to Green for help.

Aaron Green removed the top from a green fountain pen and made notes, asking questions about the coat and who found it, showing considerable interest. "It occurs to me that the new government database could solve a lot of old crimes. It's an interesting idea. As you probably know, I've been opposed to government's policy. I'm not popular with the NPP. They have men watching me..."

He replaced the top on his pen. "Thank you for bringing this to me. I believe it's something positive to campaign for. Not just your case, although I understand how important it is for you, but for other miscarriages of justice. I know the chief constable. He's a decent man...." Green paused considering his next comment. "Leave it with me." They shook hands. "Take care Mr. Reece. These are dangerous times."

Returning to the car park, Simon noticed a black Vauxhall with two men in it. The car followed him out of Carmarthen. When Simon turned left onto the main road the car was still behind him. He pulled into a lay-by and waited. His pursuers drove slowly past. Simon grabbed a petrol receipt and scribbled the car's registration number on the back.

"What did he say?" asked Sandra when he got back to Coed Mawr.

"He was quite enthusiastic. Says he'll help. He said he'd

speak to the chief constable," replied Simon. "There's something else. I think I was followed as I left his office."

"I can understand them watching Aaron Green," said Sandra. "He's been vocal about OIS abuse but why would anyone follow you?"

"I don't know but I've made a note of the car number. Do you think Gary Bridger would run a check on it?"

"I'm seeing him tomorrow. Give me the number. I'll ask," said Sandra.

Gary rang Simon the following afternoon. "The number. I had a look for you."

"And?"

"Not on the phone. I finish at six o'clock. Meet me in the Ship Inn."

Gary Bridger was sat outside when Simon arrived. "The car's registered to the OIS and there's something else." he said quietly. "The moment the registration details appeared, my computer locked up. They know I searched the number."

"You can't be sure of that."

Gary leaned forward. "You think so! I'm bloody sure of it. They know."

A crowd gathered behind a police cordon at the corner of Old Bailey and Newgate Street. Armed officers stood ready. Cables snaked away from cameras to satellite vans parked in side-streets. The world was watching and waiting. Sirens approached from the east. A convoy raced through Whitechapel, the City of London, past St. Paul's, past the Stock Exchange into Newgate Street. At its centre an armoured prison van containing one man; Masood Khan. People strained to see the approaching vehicles, to glimpse the evil man. Coffee drinkers, locked inside Cafe Nero, craned their necks to see as the vehicles thundered past. Photographers clicked hoping for a long lens scoop; a snap of Khan, the notorious terrorist, murderer of Emily Sharp and her young family.

Newspapers had already convicted Khan. He was, they said, the ringleader of a terrorist cell responsible for many murders. 'Hang Khan,' screamed the Daily News in banner headlines.

"We must let the court try the case and, if he's guilty, an appropriate sentence will be passed," declared Prime Minister Roberts. "Britain is a democracy and the rule of law will be maintained. Justice must be seen to be done."

Khan appeared in the dock, behind a bullet proof screen, flanked by four masked officers. Dressed in a green tracksuit that didn't fit he looked haggard, a frightened man, bewildered by his situation.

"Not guilty," said his barrister when the charges were read.

CHAPTER 14

Khan's trial lasted three weeks. On the last day of evidence a bright summer sun radiated warmth across London. The city sweated under a clear blue sky.

Visitors photographed themselves on the steps of St. Paul's. A street trader smiled and short-changed a tourist. Flag carrying guides hurried their charges from coaches ignoring the armed officers flanking the doors of the cathedral.

A quarter of a mile west, Masood Khan sat in the dock surrounded by armoured glass. A woman in the public gallery fanned herself. She leaned forward to see the prisoner. Beads of sweat ran down Khan's forehead. He wiped his eyes. Jurors watched, silent, as a video played of a man running through Maida Vale Underground Station with a blue rucksack on his back. A murmur ran around the court as an enhanced close up of his face was shown. Masood Khan, it was him, the man in the glass tank. Witnesses had spoken of the same man running from the explosion, of the twisted car, of mangled children's bodies. Khan's rucksack lay on the exhibit table.

"DNA recovered from the bomber's van, proves beyond any doubt - BEYOND ANY DOUBT - that Khan is the killer." announced the prosecutor.

Cameras relayed the proceedings to accredited press rooms and the outside world. Khan, the symbol of Office for Internal Security success, was on parade. This was a show trial to prove the Prime Minister's policies were working. Strongman Max Roberts was delivering his promise; the fight against terrorism was being won.

The jury returned. The foreman stood. "Guilty of all charges." The verdicts were unanimous. The court room echoed with applause as the convicted man was taken down.

James Lucas had been watching live television coverage of the trial. He switched off the monitor, returned to his desk and looked again at the data log. There, on the computer screen, was the missing video file of Khan, running through Leeds Station, carrying his blue rucksack. The log proved that the video had been doctored, photo-shopped to frame Khan. Lucas' hand hovered over the keyboard, he smiled and pressed delete.

Emlyn Hughes leafed through the report. Simon Reece and Aaron Green, the creator of Regis and that bloody politician, both high threat persons of interest. He summoned his deputy.

"I want you to find out what Reece is doing and it's time to deal with the carping from the regional parliaments. The Prime Minister is sick and tired of the continual griping about civil rights and devolved powers."

James Lucas listened to Hughes' instructions impassively. "And the policeman, Bridger?"

"His checking the registration isn't a coincidence." Hughes opened his computer and pulled up a map referenced in the report. "Look here." He pointed at the screen. "Their microchip tracks show he's met with Reece several times. He's involved."

"An accident? Maybe another bomb?"

Hughes stood up and went to the window. "Not for

Reece. We may need him in the future. Talk to him. Buy him if you have to." He smiled. "Stick and carrot - but Green is another matter. I want you to send a signal - dissent will not be tolerated."

Lucas texted Simon Reece later that day. "Call me. We need to talk."

Simon was surprised to receive the message. He rang and was put through to James Lucas.

"Simon, thanks for phoning. Can you come to London. Your claim is being assessed by the Board of Compensation and I want to discuss it with you."

"Has it been agreed? Is the government going to pay for stealing my company?"

"It's not quite that simple.... What happened wasn't my fault. The Director ordered me to sack you. I had no control over how it was done."

"So what do you want to talk about?"

"Your future and, Simon take care. Talk about stealing won't help your case. Meet me at the River Palace tomorrow 7pm. You remember it's on the Albert Embankment, we dined there before."

Simon wondered what game the deputy director of the OIS was playing? There was only one way to find out.

The metal gate was new. It opened automatically, as Simon approached, locking behind him with a click. Unseen eyes watched. "Step into the scanner and stand on the marks Mr. Reece."

Simon moved forward and placed his feet over the prints on the floor. Glass doors closed sealing him in the cubicle. A puff of air made him blink. He was being sniffed by the machine. "Step forward." Doors opened. Simon entered an inner security area. A helmeted brute of a man scanned his body, nodded and waved him towards a heavy copper clad door leading to the hotel's foyer. He entered. Noiselessly, the door slid shut.

A uniformed girl, wearing too much makeup, smiled a

greeting. "Welcome back to the River Palace Mr. Reece."

"Twelfth floor," said the metallic voice. Simon stepped out of the lift and walked along the corridor. It felt familiar, plush carpet - comfortable, inviting and yet intimidating.

The door opened. A buzz of conversation, laughter and subdued light spilled into the corridor. A grand piano, playing softly, added to the atmosphere. "Mr. Reece," said the maître d'. "This way Sir." Simon followed the man through the restaurant, past tables occupied by senior officers and their companions. A woman in a red dress was laughing, flirting with a uniformed OIS colonel. The maître d' opened a door and invited Simon to go through. The room was furnished with modern oak. A sideboard laden with polished silver stood to one side. A tapestry filled the back wall. James Lucas was seated at a dining table laid for two. He stood up. "Simon, I'm glad you've come. Nice isn't it?" He pointed to the tapestry. "St. George slaying the dragon. Appropriate, don't you think? We shall eat in here. More private. We can talk."

Simon sat down. A waiter appeared with a tray and placed two glasses containing a clear liquid on the table. "Water Sir?" Lucas nodded. The waiter poured from a jug turning the contents of the glasses cloudy.

"It's raki," said Lucas sipping his drink. "The Turks call it 'asian sutu' lion's milk."

The waiter unfolded napkins, placed them on their laps and left, closing the door as he went.

Simon studied the tapestry. Did Lucas see himself as St. George? The absurdity of a medieval St. Lucas astride a white horse, saving a fair maiden, lance in hand made him smile. "Your security people were thorough."

"Yes. A necessary precaution. Since the OIS took over the hotel it has been a high risk target.... He was Turkish you know, St. George; not British at all."

"So the patron saint of Great Britain isn't British. I didn't know that."

"I'm hungry," replied Lucas. "I've already ordered. You'll enjoy it, I'm sure."

"You said on the phone you would sort out my compensation."

The door opened and the waiter returned. He placed warm bread, olive oil and balsamic vinegar on the table.

"Relax Simon. There's no need to rush your fences." Lucas broke a piece of bread and dipped it in the oil. "Enjoy the meal. Tell me, what are you doing these days?"

"Not much. Some research into my family's background."

"Ancestry, it's an interesting subject." He took more bread. "My wife does a bit... How's Sandra?"

Of course - Lucas knew about Sandra Tate, about Simon's visits to Wales. A few mouse clicks, a look at a computer screen and he'd know it all.

The waiter returned, placed feta salads on the table and poured wine from a bottle which had been chilling on the sideboard.

Lucas tasted it. "Excellent. What is it?"

"The Montrachet Grand Cru, Sir. The maître d' selected it."

"James, you didn't fetch me here for a wine tasting evening."

Lucas waited until the waiter filled their glasses and went out. "I can get your compensation for the loss of Harland Digital approved but there's a problem I want to discuss."

"What problem?"

Lucas put down his knife and fork and looked directly at Simon. "Why did you visit Aaron Green?"

"A private family matter. I wanted his help," replied Simon.

"So you haven't discussed Regis with Green? You haven't told him how the software works or what it does?"

"Of course not. Why should I?"

The deputy director sat back in his chair and studied

Simon, "... He's a dangerous man, a troublemaker and people who associate with him should take more care."

"Thanks for the advice. You said a problem. You're going to have to explain."

"It's quite simple. I want you to work for me."

The maître d' came in followed by two waiters. They cleared away, placed clean plates on the table and served.

"What is it?" asked Simon.

"Mahmuddiye, Sir. It's a Turkish dish." said the maître d', refilling the glasses.

"Chicken Casserole with orzo and dried fruits," explained Lucas. "You'll like it." He began to eat. "Why did you ask the policeman, Bridger, to check the registration number of one of our cars?"

"It followed me when I left Green's office." Simon put down his knife and fork. "I wanted to know who it was."

"Reasonable enough I suppose. I might have done the same." Lucas reached across and refilled his glass. "Don't you like the chicken?"

"It's too sweet. I find it sickly," replied Simon. "You said you wanted me to work for you. Why? You sacked me remember."

"Yes.... That was a mistake. You weren't holding the programming up. I thought you were but I was wrong. John Hume was the spanner in the works and he still is."

"What do you mean, he still is?"

"Little things. Hume's not pulling his weight. There's an air of antipathy around him. He's always negative, making excuses for unsatisfactory work, covering up mistakes and his attitude is infecting everything."

Simon thought back to the hotel in Cambridge when they talked with the Americans. John Hume had been outspoken that day. 'Orwellian madness.' What else had he said? 'Roberts is a fascist and Britain will be a police state.' He picked at the chicken. "So sack him, like you did me."

Lucas dabbed his mouth with his napkin. "It's not that easy. The programmers worship Hume. Regis is his invention. Fire him and there would be trouble, even a revolt." He paused. "I'm offering you a way back. A consultancy, no line management responsibility; your job would be to motivate the Cambridge team. Keep them sweet."

"And John, what about him?"

Lucas pushed his plate away. "Time for dessert, I think."

There was a knock at the door. A uniformed man entered, handed Lucas a note and whispered something to him. Lucas nodded, waved the man away and read the message. "Have my car brought around," he ordered and stood up. "You will have to excuse me. Something has come up. I have urgent business to attend to. Please enjoy the rest of your meal and think about what I said. Simon, I'm offering you a chance to rebuild your life. Make the right decision." Lucas stopped in the doorway. "Call me tomorrow." Then he was gone.

The maître d' appeared, placed a small copper pot with a long wooden handle and a water jug on the table. "Mr. Lucas ordered Turkish coffee for you Sir." He poured a fresh tumbler of water and the black liquid into a cup.

"That looks strong."

"Indeed Sir."

"Why did Mr. Lucas rush off?"

"He didn't say Sir."

Simon swallowed a mouthful of water to cleanse his palate and sipped the coffee. "It's very good."

"Thank you Sir. The meal is on Mr. Lucas' account. Will there be anything else?"

"No thank you," said Simon. He finished the coffee, went downstairs and waited for the valet attendant to bring his car. It was still quite early. If there were no hold ups he'd be back in Cambridge before eleven.

GRAHAM WATKINS

CHAPTER 15

Aaron Green's evening was going well. He enjoyed Rotary Club meetings and used them to network. Tonight there was one person he particularly wanted to talk to. Vincent Kidger, Chief Constable of Dyfed-Powys, was buying a drink when Green approached.

"I'll get that Vince," said Green. "I've had a strange conversation with a man called Reece. Says he's written to you."

"Reece?" Kidger shook his head. "Don't remember the name. What did he want?"

"His parents were killed in a house fire some years ago. The arsonists were never caught. He wants a new investigation. Believes modern DNA and the national database would identify the killers."

Kidger's cell phone buzzed. He looked at a message. "Damn! I've got to go." He drained his glass. "Send me an email with the details and I'll have someone look at the case notes."

"Thanks Vince. I appreciate it," said Green as the chief constable hurried from the bar.

Aaron Green left a short while later and drove to his constituency office. He unlocked the street door and went inside unaware that he was being watched. Green fumbled in the darkness for the key to his inner office. He tried a key in the lock. It didn't fit. "Blast." He tried another. The key slid into the lock and turned easily. He went in and pressed the light switch. Fluorescent tubes flashed and flooded the room with white light. The safe where he kept his private papers was at the back of the room. Green unlocked it took out the folder marked 'TV news interview' and placed it on the desk. He removed his jacket, sat down and started to read the notes he'd made earlier. Tomorrow morning's television interview had to be just right. The facts he planned to use to denounce the NPP were imprinted in his memory. Even so, he read them again.

"I have proof the NPP leadership is corrupt which I can reveal..." He said to an imaginary audience. "No that wont' do." he muttered. "The evidence I will be putting in the public domain today is..."

Green rehearsed for an hour polishing and changing words until he was satisfied with his performance. It was later than he expected and there was still one more job he had to do. He took a sealed envelope from the safe, addressed it and posted it in the letterbox outside his office. It was time to go home. He planned to be up very early in the morning.

"Surely you aren't going to work for him?" said Sandra.

Simon was driving across Lambeth Bridge and had called Sandra from the car to discuss the meeting. "Don't you understand? It would give me access to the database. I could to use it to search for Pamela maybe find my parent's killer."

"You'd be dining with the Devil."

Simon turned right onto Millbank. "I'll buy a spoon with a long handle."

"You're going to do it aren't you... What did he say about the compensation?"

"Nothing. I never got an answer. We were interrupted. He just got up and left."

Sirens echoed in the distance. The sound grew louder. Vehicles pulled onto the pavement. A fire engine screamed past, pursued by police cars and a military armoured vehicle. "Something's happening up ahead. I'd better go. Call you later."

Simon inched slowly around Parliament Square. Emergency vehicles pushed through the jam, past Westminster Abbey and into Victoria Street. A police cordon diverted traffic north along Whitehall.

Simon turned on the radio. "No terrorist group has claimed responsibility for the attack. I'm at the scene. A car bomb has exploded outside Labour Party Campaign Headquarters. At least seven dead and multiple casualties, many of them critical," said the breathless commentator. "The OIS have secured the area and are investigating."

Aaron Green left Carmarthen along the A40. The road was quiet, the car comfortable and warm, a cocoon of soothing music. Green hummed the Titanic theme along with Celine Dion and pictured tomorrow's television appearance. He felt good. His mind drifted. Headlamps from an approaching car lit up the rear view mirror, dazzling him. A searing pain gripped the muscles in his arm. He tried to focus, to concentrate on staying on the road. He swerved. The car behind overtook. A blast of its horn and the speeding car disappeared into the night. Green concentrated on the speedometer. He was going slower now. Why couldn't he read the numbers? Why were they foggy? The car hit the verge. Airbags exploded, slamming his head back, filling the car with smoke. It tipped, nose first, into a ditch. Nausea and panic overwhelmed him. He grabbed for the door handle. Where was it? His right hand shook uncontrollably. A steel band crushed the air from his lungs. He tried to lift his arm, flailing to wipe the mucus from his nose, the sweat from his face. Desperate for air, he groped for the window switch, slid sideways, retched and rested his head against the glass. 'My Heart Will Go On,' faded into silence leaving nothing but the gentle tick of the cooling engine.

Simon watched the morning news, saw the burnt out vehicles, the masonry strewn street outside Labour Party Campaign Headquarters. Experts speculated about who, why and how. 'The attack,' they explained, 'was by terrorists, zealots determined to kill and maim.' Footage of OIS raids followed, of suspects being dragged from their homes.

The death, from a cardiac arrest, of politician Aaron Green was the last item, shoehorned between plastic pollution and gloomy weather. Simon muted the TV and phoned Harland.

"Joy Spencer please?"

"She doesn't work here anymore. Can anyone else help?" said a woman's voice.

"No, the call's personal." He hung up and sat looking out of the window. If Joy wasn't at Harland, what had happened to her? Simon was surprised. She'd been there from the very beginning, his first employee when he started the company. He pictured them working together in the tatty room he rented above Mr. Johal's shop on Russell Street. Harland was her life. She wouldn't have left without a reason.

He picked up the phone and rang her mobile number.

"Hello Simon."

"I phoned Harland. They said you'd left. Are you alright?"

She didn't answer.

"I'd like to meet up, have a chat....." Simon paused waiting for a reply. "Joy, you're not working there anymore so there's no reason not to. Tell you what, meet me at The Avery on Regent Street. I'll buy you some lunch. I'll see you in the downstairs bar at one o'clock."

"What do you want Simon?"

"I told you, to have a drink with an old friend..... Will you come?"

Simon was in the bar when Joy arrived. Her appearance shocked him. The efficient personal assistant he'd relied on had been a power dresser. Joy always came to work, perfumed, well manicured, wearing a tailored suit or an expensive dress. Now she was different. Her hair was a mess. She was wearing no makeup or perfume. Her cardigan was too large and the jeans looked dirty.

Simon pecked her on the cheek. "Pinot Grigio." He handed her a glass of wine. "I didn't think you'd come but I'm glad you have. Cheers."

Joy glanced around nervously. They studied the menu, standing at the bar.

"I haven't been here for a long time. The menu's a bit thin, typical pub grub offering," said Simon. "What would you like? I'm going for the scampi and chips."

"That's fine. I'll have the same," said Joy.

They ordered the food and went upstairs to a window table overlooking Parker's Piece. A group of youths were playing football in the park.

"It's good to see you Joy. How are you?"

"I'm fifty-three, single, unemployed and broke.... Apart for that I'm fine.... I'm sorry. That was rude of me."

There were shouts outside; a goal celebration.

A tall girl dressed in black trousers and tight fitting white shirt came up the stairs and shoved two plates on the table. "Two scampi and chips. Anything else?"

"Yes," said Simon. "we'd like two more glasses of Pinot Grigio."

"You get your drinks from the bar," said the girl and left.

"This looks fun, said Simon picking up a flowerpot containing his chips. "Haute cuisine. Shall I water them or salt and vinegar them, Madame?"

Joy managed a momentary smile.

"Why did Lucas sack you?"

"He didn't. I couldn't stick it any longer. I quit. The atmosphere was toxic. John Hume and Lucas hate each other and Lucas doesn't understand the business. He's vindictive, a bully, runs the place like a gulag. Everyone despises him." She stared out of the window. "He wanted me to spy on the others, to report back."

Simon tipped chips onto his plate, placed the flowerpot at the end of the table and sprinkled vinegar on his meal. "He's asked me to go back, he says to lift morale."

Joy snorted. "You'd be a fool to go back to Harland. The place is evil. It's not what the people do there, it's what they make possible; what Regis makes possible. I've got to say it, Simon. You and John created a monster."

They finished eating. "What will you do?"

"I'm sick of Cambridge. My flat's up for sale," said Joy. "I have a sister in Warwick. I'll go there... And you? Will you go back to Harland?"

"I don't know," answered Simon. "I haven't decided."

That evening the Prime Minister addressed the nation. Emlyn Hughes watched the broadcast from his office; Max Roberts condemning the London bombing, promising the perpetrators would be found and punished.

The Prime Minister sat behind a desk, presidential style, a union flag draped neatly behind. "This is war. And, there will be casualties - but we will win. Gainsayers and terrorist sympathisers are enemies who will be dealt with."

The phone rang. Emlyn Hughes picked it. "C.J. Hunt, yes, put him through... C.J. where's my money?"

"Two hundred thousand was transferred to Cayman National Bank last week," drawled the American. "It should be in your account. Have you checked?"

"Of course I bloody well checked. It wasn't there yesterday. I tried to log in this morning and it won't let me. Says the password I'm using is incorrect."

"Sorry Emlyn, we've paid. What do you expect me to do?.. Did you change the password?"

"I haven't changed anything. The password is the one you gave me in Houston."

"Get your technical people to have a look at it." said C.J. barely concealing his enjoyment.

"If you're cheating me you'll regret it." spat Hughes.

"Relax Emlyn. We'll check out the account from this end and Emlyn, don't ever threaten me again."

Hughes slammed the receiver down, composed himself and telephoned James Lucas. "What's happening with Reece? Did he accept?"

"No director. I spoke to him this afternoon. He's not coming back to Harland. I'm glad. I don't trust him."

"You don't trust him! I should hope not. It's your job not to trust people." Spit ran down Hughes' chin. "He's made his choice. Deal with him. It's time to move to the next phase. Have you prepared the reports for the media?"

"They're ready for release Director," replied Lucas.

"Good. These are high profile people who can cause trouble. There must be no mistakes."

CHAPTER 16

Simon put the newspaper on the table. "Have you seen this? William Fearn's taking a chance claiming that closing the Welsh Assembly and Scottish Parliament is a crude power grab. He's calling the government crooks."

"Fearn was arrested this morning. It was just on the radio. Wales News has been closed," said Sandra. "It said they have proof he's a traitor, a mouthpiece working for the Russians."

Sandra picked up the paper and read Fearn's piece.

WELSH AND SCOTTISH PARLIAMENTS
SUSPENDED
Abolition of Legislatures Sparks Fiery Row
By Political Editor William Fearn

Welsh and Scottish voters will no longer have a say in their internal affairs.

The sudden draconian move announced by the government comes into immediate effect.

Documents, leaked exclusively to Wales News, reveals secret NPP plans were suppressed before the general election.

Claims by Assembly Members that the changes are unlawful were dismissed by the government last night. 'Regional talking shops

*are a waste of taxpayer's money,' said Quentin Abbot - newly
appointed Minister of State. 'The National People's Party represents
everyone. There is no place for local pressure groups.'*

*Welsh Labour Party Leader, Ray Wilding, condemned the move
as, 'A step towards a one party state.'*

*'I've been manhandled from my office by OIS thugs,' shouted
Assembly Member David Walters as he was removed from the
building. Onlookers reported he was covered in blood. The AM, a
critic of the NPP, was later seen being forced into a police van by
armed officers.*

*Demonstrators, protesting against the closure of the Welsh
Assembly, were dispersed with tear gas and baton rounds.....*

William Fearn's story made other explosive claims.
Someone inside the government was leaking confidential
files. Persons of interest to the OIS were being named for
public ridicule, important political figures smeared,
campaigns of misinformation and other dirty tricks
planned by the government. The paper's coverage pulled
no punches. Fearn had a mole in high places.

Elsewhere the media stuck to the press releases
prepared by the government. Regional assemblies were
being suspended they said because they had been
infiltrated by extremist sympathisers and troublemakers
working to undermine national security. Lucas' propaganda
was being repeated as commanded.

"Are you still going to work for Lucas?" asked Sandra.

"No. I told him yesterday. He wanted to use me."
Simon filled his coffee cup. "I don't like the man. He's
going to crucify John Hume."

"He's your friend. You should warn him."

Simon thought back to the day he was fired when John
Hume had turned his back and walked away.

There was a knock at the door.

"That'll be Gary," said Sandra. "Let him in. I'll make
another cup."

Simon opened the door and invited Gary Bridger into

the kitchen.

The policeman put his hat on the table and scowled. "I've been hauled up in front of the chief constable. Warned off. I told you they knew."

"Warned off!" said Simon. "What do you mean?"

"I checked the car registration, you remember. He just said be careful. That was it." Gary shrugged. "He didn't say much else. Didn't seem interested. He just dismissed it as nothing. Then he talked about Aaron Green's death. Said it was strange that the OIS were there when he crashed and wouldn't let the ambulance crew go near the body. I don't think he's got any time for the OIS."

"Did you see the news?" asked Simon.

"About the Welsh Assembly?" Gary nodded. "There's going to be a big demonstration in Cardiff on Saturday. It's going to get nasty. All police leave has been cancelled."

Simon's mobile phone rang. "Mr. Reece? This is the janitor. I'm sorry to have to tell you, your flat's been broken into. The police are here now."

"Give it to me," said a voice in the background. "Mr. Reece, this is Sergeant Francis. I need to you come back to Cambridge to establish what's been taken."

"Is there much mess?.... Yes. Thank you I'll be there this evening, about eight o'clock."

"What's the matter, Simon?" asked Sandra. "You look dreadful."

"My flat's been burgled. I've got to get back to Cambridge."

Simon pushed the door open and stepped over broken glass. Sergeant Francis, grey haired and close to retirement, was in the sitting room. A constable, fresh faced and enthusiastic, sat opposite. They stood up. Simon looked around. His flat had been wrecked, furniture overturned, possessions strewn across the floor. He felt numb and angry. He wanted to lash out, to punch someone. The burglars had ripped the television from its mounting. The wall safe was open, its contents gone. Simon's laptop was also missing.

"What was in the safe?" asked Sergeant Francis.

"Some papers and a couple of thousand in cash."

"Do you have backups?" asked the constable, "for the computer?"

Simon nodded.

"The crime's been flagged by the Office for Internal Security," said Sergeant Francis. "You must be important Mr. Reece. A burglary is normally a local police matter. The OIS are taking over the investigation."

"Who do you think did it?"

"Not for me to say, Sir. Not now the OIS are in charge." Sergeant Francis picked up a broken glass object and held the heavy pieces together. "Pity." He placed it on the table. "Interesting ornament."

"It was an entrepreneur of the year trophy," said Simon quietly.

"Yours Sir, is it?"

Two uniformed OIS men appeared in the doorway. "We'll take over."

Sergeant Francis nodded to his colleague. "Nice to meet you Mr. Reece. Goodbye and good luck."

The sergeant and his side-kick squeezed past the OIS men and left.

"You need to come with us Mr. Reece," said the taller OIS officer. "Our locksmith will secure your flat and a team will be here shortly to gather evidence."

The second OIS man moved quietly around the room and stood behind Simon. His breath stank of garlic. There was a 'beep' as he scanned Simon's microchip.

"It's him," said the man. He pulled Simon's hands back and tried to handcuff them. The manacles locked onto one hand.

Simon pulled away. "What the hell are you doing?"

There was a searing pain in his chest. His body went rigid. Simon tried to cry out but no sound came. He fell to the ground shaking uncontrollably. His muscles throbbed. His testicles felt like they were exploding.

The taller officer holstered his taser. "Cuff him and bring him to the car."

GRAHAM WATKINS

CHAPTER 17

The car sped north from Cambridge. Simon was in the back wedged between the officers. His arms, still handcuffed, cramped and pressed against the metal barbs of the taser hooked in his back. He tried to move to ease the spasms of pain but there was no relief. Numbed by the electric shock, his body ached. Simon tried to focus, to think but his mind refused. He lost consciousness. The vehicle turned off the main road. They were heading into the fens. Simon woke with a start. The car was stationary. The driver's window was open. He was talking to someone. Ahead was a high fence and gates. Armed men stood guard. The gates opened. The car moved forward to a second set of gates. They drove through and continued on, passing derelict military buildings, nissen huts a control tower and bunkers. The vehicle stopped at a large hangar. The men pulled Simon from the car. He tried to stand but his legs buckled. They half dragged him to a large room. A metal lampshade, hanging from the ceiling, cast a pool of yellow light on a table. Faceless men watched from the shadows.

"Simon Reece," said the taller OIS man and unfastened the handcuffs. "Had to taser him. You'll need to remove the darts."

A pair of pliers was produced. They leaned Simon across the table and held him down. He cried out as the barbs ripped free. Simon was stripped and given an orange boiler-suit.

"Row sixteen, cell eleven," said a voice. Guards manhandled Simon into the aircraft hangar. He looked around through half closed eyes and saw cages, hundreds of them. Sullen eyes watching from every one. He stumbled.

A guard kicked him. "Get up."

They pushed him into a cage. The gate slammed, locking itself shut with a loud click. A metal framed bed was at the back of the cage. Near it stood a steel toilet and a sink, a wooden seat and fixed to the bars a metal shelf. Simon sat on the chair and glanced at the prisoner on his left. Its occupant, a timid, weasel looking man turned away, refusing to make eye contact. A big man on the other side was on his bed and looked asleep.

Sodium lights, high about the cages, barely pierced the gloom. Simon heard a squeak and the clatter of metal. An old man was, moving along the gangway, pushing a trolley. He stopped at each cage and pushed a metal tray through the bars. The old man looked directly at Simon, smiled a toothless grin, slipped a tray onto Simon's shelf and shuffled on. The congealed food on the tray looked revolting.

"If you don't want it, pass it over," whispered the sleeping man.

"What's your name?" asked Simon. "How long have you been here?"

"Keep your voice down," hissed the man. "Petch. I've been here three weeks."

Simon held the tray through the slot in the front of his cage.

Petch reached for it and started to eat. "Thanks," he muttered between mouthfuls.

"Where are we?" asked Simon.

"High Lingham detention camp. Used to be an airfield."

The whispered conversation continued, their heads pressed close to the bars. Simon told how he was taken from his flat.

"I used to be a paratrooper," said Petch. "Came out of the army and joined the OIS. A lot of soldiers did the same."

"You're OIS! So why are you in here?"

"I did something stupid. I spoke out. Said what we were doing was wrong. Should have kept my mouth shut. Followed orders." The big man shrugged. "It was supposed to be an ordinary arrest. Four of us to collect a guy called Cooper. I don't know what he'd done. It was early morning when we went in. My job was to smash the door down. It only took one hit with the ram and we were in the hall. There was a woman, a pretty thing she was, on the stairs. The sergeant grabbed her hair and pulled her down. She screamed." Petch paused and took a deep breath. "I'm not soft. I've done two tours in Afghanistan. Seen plenty of death and brutality but this was here, in England. It was different."

"What happened?"

"He clubbed her with his gun. Not once, again and again. He just kept hitting her. Cooper charged down the stairs. He was a puny little man, all skin and bone wearing nothing but pyjama bottoms. He never had a chance." Petch sniffed. "I shot him. He landed beside the girl. He was still alive."

They heard footsteps. A guard was approaching along the gangway. Petch moved away from the bars and lay on his bed. The guard passed without stopping.

The big man came back. "The sergeant ordered me to kill them both. 'Shoot them in the head,' he said. I couldn't do it. I told him it was murder, it was wrong. He grinned and put two rounds in Cooper's head and then did the same to the girl," said Petch and shook his head. "When I spoke out, said what he'd done, they said I'd disobeyed orders and brought me to this stinking hole.

"We're all here, enemies of the state. Eight hundred men. Honest policemen, terrorists, politicians, people who drop litter, anyone the OIS dislike or are afraid of. Anyone they can't control with their microchips and that bloody database, Regis." The big man sniffed. "So, why are you here?"

"I created Regis. Well, my company did and now I won't help them, I guess I must be an enemy."

"You! You invented Regis." Petch grinned. "You bloody well deserve to be in here."

There was a load crack and the lights went out.

The undertaker, in his long coat and top hat, walked ahead of the cortège, each pace measured, precise, swinging his black cane in solemn accompaniment. He stopped at the main road, turned, bowed to the hearse and stepped into the passenger seat. Police officers stopped the traffic, clearing the way for the funeral procession. The cortège crossed the river and into the town. People threw flowers in the road. Shoppers stopped to stare. "Who's in the coffin?" they wondered. Others hurried on unconcerned.

Silent mourners watched the coffin being carried, shoulder high, through the lych-gate and into the church. Aaron Green had been a popular assembly member, well respected. His sudden death had stirred public interest. A television crew was interviewing onlookers.

"So young. He was a good man," said a woman. She spoke quietly, reverently.

"He stood for what was right. Told the truth," said another.

Vincent Kidger was in uniform, attending in his official capacity as chief constable but he was also there to pay his respects to a fellow Rotarian, a man he considered no more than a passing acquaintance. Kidger walked the short distance from his official car and moved through the crowd. A television reporter pushed her microphone towards him.

"Chief Constable, will you be investigating Aaron Green's death?" He smiled at her and went into the church.

St. John's was full. Another cameraman was setting up ready to film the service. Green, defender of ordinary people, was dead but not yet forgotten.

Kidger walked along the aisle to the front, took his place behind the family and nodded to the mayor. He picked up the order of service and frowned; four hymns.

"Aaron Green was a generous man," declared the bishop. Her amplified words echoed around the church. Someone coughed. A chair scraped the floor at the back of the church. "He was a man who would help anyone. A man so full of life with a huge heart and yet he was only forty-two when God called him from us. I remember..."

Green's widow sobbed.

Kidger's eyes wandered. He studied the stained glass window; saintly images glorified in the sun light and, in the bottom corner, a red stain - the flames of hell. He glanced at his watch.

The bishop was still speaking. "Why? I hear you ask did God take a good man from us? A stout hearted man, who had so much to give..."

Kidger remembered the last time he saw Green and wondered what good deed he was doing then?

Aaron Green had asked him to help. An arson attack he'd said! Priest, Reeves, Reece? Was that it, Reece?

The chief constable followed Green's widow and her children from the church and stood beside them watching the coffin slide into the hearse.

"I'm so sorry Mrs Green," he said quietly. "I knew your husband well. If there's anything I can do."

She stared at him, ashen faced.

"This way Mrs Green," said the undertaker and guided

her to a funeral car.

Kidger straightened his cap and strode purposefully along the road to where his driver waited. "Headquarters," he ordered. He got in the car and phoned his assistant. "I want a search of cold cases made. Pull any that have the name Reeves or Reece, particularly if they involve an arson attack."

Sandra had heard nothing from Simon for more than a week and was worried. She'd sent texts, left phone messages - nothing. Where was he? Why wasn't he returning her calls, answering her messages?

She phoned Gary. "It's Simon. I've been calling him. He won't speak to me." She sniffed. "I don't know what to do."

"Have you argued... Fallen out over something?"

"No," she whined. "Have you spoken to him? Did I do something wrong?"

"I'll come over."

Sandra was composed when Gary arrived but her red eyes betrayed the tears. They sat drinking coffee in a gloomy mood of unspoken, unanswered questions.

"Has he dumped me?"

Gary leaned forward and kissed her cheek.

"What are you doing?" She pulled away. "Don't."

"I'm sorry... I..." He touched his mouth. "You like him very much."

Her unfocused eyes stared at the wall. "I don't know what to do."

"Do you want me to find him?"

She nodded. "Would you?"

"I'll get my laptop from the car."

Gary used his police computer to log into Regis. "Here it is," he said opening Simon's file.

Sandra'd not seen the database before. There, in front of her, was the government record of a man, the man who, she thought, had abandoned her. His mug-shot, taken

136

when he was micro-chipped, looked back at her, unsmiling and stiff. She moved closer to the screen brushing against a mug. It fell from the table and shattered on the floor, scattering shards of china. "Shit," she said and bent to gather the pieces. She dropped the bits in the bin and went to the sink.

"Have you cut yourself?" asked Gary. "Let me see." He rinsed her finger, wrapped it in a twist of kitchen paper and cupped her hand in his. "Hold it tight. The bleeding will soon stop."

"Thanks." She hesitated then let her hand slip through his fingers.

Gary returned to the computer. "That's odd." He pointed to the breadcrumb trail on the screen. "That's the track left by Simon as he went to his flat but look at the time. He only stayed for a few minutes."

"What does it mean?" asked Sandra as she sat down beside him.

"If there was a burglary he wouldn't have just left," said Gary. "It doesn't make sense."

"Where did he go?"

"He drove north east." Gary scrolled the map, following the trail. "It's gone. The track just ends."

"I don't understand."

They sat looking at the screen.

"Something terrible's happened to him."

"We don't know that," said Gary. "There'll be a simple explanation. His microchip's broken or something."

"So why hasn't he rung?"

"I don't know... Tell you what. I'll ring Cambridgeshire police," suggested Gary and reached for his phone.

"This is Constable Bridger of Dyfed Powys Police. My collar number's 51682. I'm making enquiries into the disappearance of a man named Simon Reece last heard of returning to his home reportedly burgled on the 16th of this month."

"You need to speak to Sergeant Francis. The burglary

was his case," said the control room operator. "I'll put you through."

"You say you're a policeman. What's your interest in Mr. Reece?" asked the sergeant abruptly.

"Simon's a friend of mine and he's missing," said Gary. "I understand you asked him to return to Cambridge because of the burglary."

"...Reece never showed up at the flat. Sorry I can't help you. I've been taken off the case."

"So who's in charge of the investigation? Let me speak to them."

"I told you. I can't help."

"What's he saying?" asked Sandra.

Gary looked at her and frowned. "He's hung up."

CHAPTER 18

Max Roberts sat at the end of a conference table, scanned the documents and frowned. "Why bring them to me?"

James Lucas' mouth was dry. "I thought you should know Prime Minister, about the money."

"So you're saying your boss, the director of the OIS is taking backhanders from the Americans. He's accepting bribes. He's in the American's pocket!"

"The account at Cayman National Bank proves it. Look at the statement. Hughes was paid two million dollars up front and was receiving two hundred thousand a month. There's nearly three million in the account."

"What do you mean was? Have the payments stopped?"

Lucas relaxed. "No Prime Minister, the payments are still being made by the Americans but Hughes isn't able to access the account. I've changed the password and locked him out. He can't touch the money."

Max Roberts sat back in his chair and studied the young man in front of him. "I see." He rubbed his chin. "This is a serious matter. Have you spoken to him? Does he know the password's changed?"

"I haven't spoken to him. If he's tried to access the

account recently he'll know there's a problem." Lucas smiled. "I thought it better to bring this to you than try and handle it on my own."

"I'm glad you did and I appreciate your loyalty. Loyalty is so important. It deserves to be rewarded. You agree?"

Lucas nodded.

The Prime Minister closed the file and patted it with his hand. "Leave this with me. I'll deal with your boss." He pressed a button on the desk. The meeting was over.

"One more thing," said the Prime Minister. "The new password, give it to me." He waited until the OIS deputy director shut the door and picked up the telephone.

"Emlyn, you bastard, you've been up to your old tricks again. We need to talk and a word in your ear; your deputy, Lucas, keep an eye on him. The disloyal little shit just tried to stick a dagger in your back."

Simon Reece lost track of time. His only reference was the yellow glow of sodium lighting. Each morning there would be a crack and the lights would come on. Each night they would go off. On the eighth or ninth day the guards came for the man in the next cage; the man who averted his eyes and refused to speak. He whimpered like a frightened child when they took him. It was the first and only sound Simon heard him make.

"Where will they take him?" whispered Simon.

Petch shook his head and drew his outstretched fingers across his throat.

A new prisoner arrived to replace the silent man, a Pakistani youth, wide eyed and terrified. Fear had loosened his tongue. He was Awan Jarwar, he said, from Luton. "They took me from my father's house. I've done nothing. They hit my mother."

"Be quiet," hissed Petch. "A guard's coming."

"The men beat me for nothing. Look!" He lifted his shirt to show the bruises. "LOOK."

The guard was closer now.

"Shut up," spat Petch through his teeth.

The youth was crying. He clawed at the cage. "Let me out. I haven't done anything."

The guard pushed a stick through the bars. The boy screamed and collapsed. He lay on the floor, clutching his chest, sobbing like a child.

"Silence," said the guard. He stepped over to Petch's cage.

"Poor sod," whispered Petch. "Did you have to do that Monk?"

"We're nearly there Petch. I'll tell you when." whispered the guard and strolled away.

"Cattle prod," said Petch quietly. "That's why nobody makes any noise."

"What did he say to you?" asked Simon.

Petch ignored the question.

That night Simon asked again. "You called that guard Monk. What did he mean when he said, 'Were nearly there'?"

Petch hesitated. "Monk, did I? You shouldn't have heard that."

Gary and Sandra drove to Cambridge following the trail, created by Simon's tracker. They stopped at a supermarket where Gary bought a roll of kitchen foil.

"What's that for?" asked Sandra as they walked back to the car.

"It's to hide us from prying eyes." He unlocked to doors. "Get in. I'll show you."

He opened the foil and tore off a length. "Which arm is your microchip in?"

"My left one, why?"

"Take your jacket off and hold your arm out straight."

He wrapped the foil around her arm and then did the same to his.

"It's a trick crooks use so they aren't detected. The metal hides the microchip's signal. Be careful as you pull you jacket on. You mustn't rip the foil."

They drove on, following Simon's track to a remote country road in East Anglia.

"It ends about half a mile over there," said Sandra and pointed to some large buildings.

Gary pulled off the road into a gateway and they got out of the car. "It looks like a war time aerodrome," he said and fetched binoculars from the car. "I can see vehicles moving about." He passed the field glasses to Sandra.

She leaned on the gate to steady the glasses. "There are men by the fence. They're carrying rifles. Do you think it's some sort of camp?"

Behind them, a quiet drone, almost unnoticeable at first, was getting louder. A light aircraft flew low over their heads. It landed and taxied towards a hanger. The pilot climbed out.

"He's pointing at us," said Sandra.

A vehicle sped across the tarmac, towards the gates.

"Sandra, get in the car, NOW! We have to go. Get in." Gary revved the engine, slammed the car into reverse. It shot into the lane. He crunched into first gear, spun the steering wheel and accelerated away. "The man in the plane must have seen us as he flew over."

Gary Bridger didn't slow down until they reached Cambridge.

"Do you think Simon's there, at that camp?" asked Sandra as she peeled foil from her arm.

"Yes. I'm sure he is."

"What can we do?"

"I don't know," said Gary.

CHAPTER 19

Vincent Kidger's assistant placed two buff folders on his desk. "I've checked the computer records. Nothing with the name Reeves or Reece and these are the only cold cases involving arson attacks."

"Thanks Vivian. A coffee would be nice."

Vivian went out and shut the door. The chief constable opened the first folder and read the case notes. The unsolved crime was an arson attack in 1997 on The Duke's Head, a public house in Llanelli, possibly gang related, said the report. Strong suspicions and two suspects but not enough evidence to prosecute the case. Kidger scanned the investigating officer's statement. The fire gutted the building but no one was hurt.

This wasn't the case Aaron Green was talking about. Kidger picked up the second folder. It contained statements and records of a forest fire in 2006. The fire on the Brecon Beacons, which was started deliberately, had spread destroying three thousand hectares of mature timber and a farmhouse. The arsonists, believed to be teenagers, were never identified. Again, there were no casualties. Green said the man's parents were killed in the blaze so this fire wasn't the one he spoke about at the

Rotary Club meeting.

Losing interest Kidger, wrote, 'Return to archive' on a yellow post-it note and put the cold case files in his out tray. Other, more pressing matters, demanded his attention.

Vivian returned and placed a tray with coffee and chocolate biscuits on his desk. She poured a cup of coffee and collected the files from the out tray. "Not what you were looking for?"

"No," replied the chief constable, picking up a biscuit. "Doesn't matter. It's probably not important."

"You've a superintendant's meeting at four o'clock. The briefing notes are on your desk."

"Yes I've already reviewed them. Inform the county commanders I want them at the meeting will you Vivian? Oh! And the director of Intelligence."

"More demands for recruits from the OIS?"

"They're looking for experienced investigating officers."

Vivian nodded. She understood the pressure her boss was under to hit targets with ever reducing resources. He looked increasingly tired these days she thought as she went out and shut the door.

Curious about the cold cases the Chief Constable had asked about, Vivian did some investigating of her own. She had a vague recollection that she'd heard or read the name Reece somewhere. Vivian opened an enquiry in the correspondence master file and typed the name in the search box. Moments later a document containing the name Reece showed up. It was a letter she'd written replying to a Mr. Reece concerning a cold case enquiry he'd made. His original letter had been scanned and was also in the file. Vivian printed them both and placed them on the chief constable's desk. Then she sent a request to records to retrieve the archive files for the 1980 arson attack at Coed Mawr. They were delivered to the chief constable the following morning.

Gary Bridger waited outside the Chief Constable's office. He picked up a copy of 'Police Magazine', skimmed through it and replaced it with the other magazines on the coffee table in front of him.

The chief constable's assistant looked up from her desk and smiled at him. Her phone buzzed.

"Send him in, Vivian."

Gary checked his tie was straight and knocked on the door.

"Come."

Kidger didn't look up or greet him.

"Constable Bridger, you filed a missing person's report on a Simon Reece." The chief constable leafed through the report. "Do you know him?"

"Yes Sir. Well vaguely, he's an acquaintance, a friend of Sandra Tate. Miss Tate reported him missing."

"Miss Tate, yes I've read her statement." Vincent Kidger sat back in his chair and studied the young constable. "Do you know who he is?"

"He's a businessman. Computers I think."

Kidger smiled. "Computers you think! What else do you know about him? Do you know he's been trying to get an old arson case reopened?"

"Yes Sir."

"This is what he wants investigated." Kidger tapped a folder on his desk. "He wants to find out who killed his parents. Is that why he's gone missing do you think?"

"I don't know."

"According to the case notes Sergeant Hughes was the investigating officer." Kidger opened the file. "You know who he is, Don't you?"

"Yes Sir. He's the Director of the OIS."

Kidger sat back and rubbed his neck. "Your father was with Hughes on the night of the fire... I don't know what's going on but you're in it up to your neck. Tell me about the registration check you did on the OIS car."

"Simon asked me to do it. He said the car followed him when he left Aaron Green's office."

"It's Simon now is it?" Kidger raised his voice. "Someone you say you know vaguely, an acquaintance, asks you to use police resources to check out a car. I could sack you for that... Now, I want the truth."

Simon Reece was woken by the food trolley rumbling along the concrete floor. He opened one eye. A meal tray was passed to Petch but there was something else. Simon glimpsed it for just a second; something white, a small piece of paper changed hands and then vanished.

He waited until they'd eaten. "I saw it," he whispered.

"Saw what?" said Petch.

"A note. He slipped it to you."

"You mean this." Petch grinned, tore the note up and dropped it into his toilet. "It's tomorrow tonight. I'll be saying goodbye. I'm getting out of here."

"Do you mean you're going to break out?" Simon moved closer to the bars. "How?"

"Simple. I'm going to drive through the gates."

"Take me with you."

Petch stretched out on his bed and put his hands behind his head. "Why should I?"

"Because you need me. I can help. I know where we can hide, somewhere Regis will never find us."

"Nah, you'd slow me down," said Petch and turned his back towards Simon.

The following morning Petch beckoned to Simon. "Where's this place you know?"

"It's a friend's house, in the country, miles from anywhere. We'd be safe there... Do you have a better plan? Where were you're going to run to?"

Petch shook his head. "No. You're right. I hadn't thought it through. I'll get us out but, I'm warning you, your safe house had better be good."

Sandra Tate listened carefully to Gary's account of his meeting with the chief constable. "Tell me again. What did he tell you to do?"

"That's the thing. It made no sense. I told him everything, about the fire, the coat, how we tracked Simon's microchip to the airfield in East Anglia, about his involvement with Regis. I even told him how Hatchet Hughes blackmailed my father. He just sat and listened. He didn't react. There was no surprise, he didn't smile or frown. Nothing. At the end he thanked me for being honest and said he would consider the matter."

"Do you think he'll report you to the OIS?"

"No and I'll tell you why." He paused. "As I was leaving he told me to be very careful. 'Dark forces are at work.' Those were his words."

GRAHAM WATKINS

CHAPTER 20

Lucas waited for the eruption signalling the demise of Director Hughes and - hopefully - his own promotion. Not a word.

Another day of waiting... and still nothing.

Totally baffling! Roberts had the evidence proving Emlyn Hughes was an embezzler so what the hell was he doing?

The Prime Minister needed a nudge, a startling nudge. It was time to force the issue. Lucas scanned the incriminating documents he'd kept in his safe and saved the files to his laptop.

He left Harland Digital carrying a laptop bag and drove into town. It was market day and the streets were crowded. Lucas, parked, walked quickly to a phone shop and bought a cheap pay as you go mobile. "Put ten pounds of credit on it," he said and paid with cash.

As he was leaving the assistant called out, "Your bag, Sir. You've forgotten your bag." She pointed to the floor in front of the counter. Lucas swallowed, retrieved the case containing his laptop and scurried out without a word. He hurried to a small anonymous cafe.

The girl behind the counter was playing a game on her

mobile phone. She slipped the phone into her pocket. "A flat white and ginger cake. Anything else?"

Lucas shook his head.

"Four pounds sixty."

The deputy director handed her a five pound note, took his change and moved to a table at the back of the cafe. The girl went back to her phone. He booted the laptop and sipped coffee. The mobile phone in his pocket buzzed. It was linking with the computer. He re-read a draft email, written earlier and attached the images of the files from his safe. The blue-tooth light blinked and stayed on. The laptop was talking to the phone, grabbing the email and the images.

A tap of the finger and there... gone... that'll force the PM into action. Hughes' Cayman Bank statement was with the editor of The Daily Globe. The Globe would hit this big! Lucas smiled but he wasn't finished yet. He forwarded a copy of the email to the leader of the Labour Party. Lucas closed the laptop, picked up the cake and took a bite. It tasted sickly, a desiccated mix that was impossible to swallow.

He dropped the phone into the River Cam. There would, he believed, be no link to him, no evidence of his treachery.

Back at Lingham three OIS guards were having a game of poker and a quiet drink in a small remote building, away from the hangers.

Monk refilled their glasses and returned to the table. "Not my lucky night," he said placing drinks in front of his new friends. The game continued. Monk was losing but he didn't seem to care. They were all drunk and having a good time.

The man, on Monk's left, dropped his cards on the floor and tried, unsuccessfully to pick them up. He fell off his chair, farted loudly and started to laugh. The others joined in laughing raucously, uncontrollably.

The second guard wiped his eyes. He giggled, tried to stand and flopped back into his seat.

Monk looked at his companions, one asleep on the floor and the second head down on the table. Both had passed out. The Rohypnol tablets had done their work. He moved silently around the table, stood behind the seated man, put a plastic strap around the man's throat and squeezed, twisting it tight, until he was sure the man was dead.

A groan, a whimper. The man on the floor moved, tried to get up. Monk, moved quickly, smashing his head down on the concrete. He turned him on his back, sat on his chest and started to strangle him with his hands. The man fought back, eyes wide, kicking out, twisting, turning - desperate to live.

The body was still when Monk released his grip. He was breathing heavily and sweating. He sat by the corpse to recover. Then, he got to his feet, laid the bodies side by side, picked up the money on the table and left, locking the door behind him.

"Well, can we use the story?" asked the editor. The evening editorial meeting was electric. This was big.

Les Romney, the *Globe's* veteran political correspondent knew the anonymous tip off was libellous but it was dynamite. "We've got to use it but we can't name Hughes."

"I agree," said the editor. "We're going to break the story, front page. It's our splash for tomorrow. I want a double deck headline. Make it big. Les, speak to Downing Street. See if you can get a denial."

"What about a spread? This is way better than the Nigerian corruption story."

"No," said the editor. "We don't have enough yet. We'll do a spread when the name's public. Keep the centre pages as they are."

Before the story went to print it was checked by the paper's lawyer. "Has the Prime Minister ordered an investigation?"

"I've no idea," replied Romney. "Does it matter? Roberts would look a fool if he denied it. Call it creative journalism."

The lawyer snorted. "You can't print it."

"That's my decision," said the editor. "You advise what we can print and I decide."

The story appeared in a late edition the following morning.

SECURITY CHIEF BRIBED
MILLIONS BY USA
PM Probes Shock Treachery Claim

Secret papers obtained exclusively by the Daily Globe claim Prime Minister Max Roberts has been alerted to devastating espionage by a bribed top OIS official.

A high-level officer alleges that a trusted colleague has been paid at least three million pounds from the USA for potentially sabotaging the economy by selling state secrets.

He has also provided Cayman Bank documents to confirm his claim. Payments are apparently still pouring into the hidden bank account at the rate of two hundred thousand a month and our source states the impact on the UK economy is 'potentially devastating'.

A Downing Street spokesman refused to comment last night.

The Globe asked if the PM was acting on the allegations and was told: "You've already been told ... no comment."

Roberts, however, has ordered an immediate investigation.

A loud bang echoed around the hanger as the lights went out. Eight hundred cage doors swung open. Prisoners rushed from their cells, pushing, tripping, fighting their way towards the hanger doors. A siren screamed. Men covered their ears to block the pain. Others beat guards, shocking them with prods, driving them into the night air.

Petch ran from the hanger towards an OIS car. Simon followed. The driver was waving. "Come on Petch," he shouted. There were shots. A bullet hit the side of the car. More shots. Men were falling. A prisoner opened the car door. Petch slammed his head against bodywork and pushed him aside He climbed in, pulled Simon into the car and tried to shut the door but there was an arm in the way.

"It's Awan the kid from Luton," gasped Simon. Crack! A bullet hit the car. He dragged the boy in. The driver hit the accelerator. The door shut with a bang.

The driver was wearing an OIS uniform. It was the guard Petch had spoken to.

"Who is he?" asked Simon. The car hit a bank, took off across a ditch and landed heavily.

"He's Monk, a mate of mine from the Paras," said Petch. "We were in Afghanistan together. Did you get 'em, Monk?"

"Yeah two, like you said. They're in a hut at the end of the runway."

"How are we going to get out of the airfield?" asked Simon.

Petch grinned. "We're going to drive through the main gate like royalty."

Monk parked behind a derelict building. The men hurried inside. The building was dark and stank; a sweet, putrid smell. Monk turned on a torch and placed it on a chair. Two OIS men were on the floor.

"How'd you kill them?" asked Petch.

"Date rape," smirked Monk. "Take off your shirt."

Petch unbuttoned his shirt and removed it. "What about these two?" asked Monk. "We can't leave them here. Not alive. They know too much."

Petch's torso shone in the lamplight. "You're still clean Monk. They don't know you're involved. He can have yours," he pointed to Simon.

"And the other one? They're not part of the plan Petch. Let's keep to what we agreed. Just the two of us." Monk pulled a plastic strap from his pocket. "I'll do it now." He moved towards the young Asian. The boy backed away, towards the corner of the room and whimpered.

"Don't kill the boy, please." interrupted Simon. "He's done nothing wrong."

"Leave him." Despite his size, Petch moved quickly forcing himself between Monk and the boy. "We can use him."

Monk hesitated. "How?"

"I've an idea. Did you bring the scanner?"

Monk nodded.

"Get it," ordered Petch. He started to undress one of the dead men. "Come here Simon. Get his clothes off."

They undressed the corpses.

"Oh God, he stinks," said Simon. "He's shit himself."

"He's dead," snapped Petch. "What did you expect? Monk, give me the scanner."

He scanned an arm. The instrument registered. Monk unfolded a lock knife and dug into the cold flesh, probing. "I've got it." He held up the dead man's microchip.

Monk produced a small bottle of alcohol and wiped the blade. He scanned Petch's arm. There was a beep. Monk drew a cross. "This is going to hurt."

"Bring the torch over here." ordered Petch. Simon held the lamp up.

"Hold the bloody torch still," ordered Monk.

"Fuck, fuck, fuck," muttered Petch as the knife went in.

Monk twisted the blade and prized out Petch's chip. He cleaned and bandaged the cut folded the dead man's chip into the last turn of the dressing."It's your turn. Get your shirt off."

"Sod that," replied Simon. "You're not cutting me."

"Take it off," ordered Monk. "Bite on this." He tied the sleeve into a knot, stuffed it into Simon's mouth and began to probe. Silent tears ran down Simon's face as his chip was cut out and the wound bandaged.

They dressed in the dead men's clothes and ran outside.

Petch was the last to leave, tossing a petrol soaked rag into the building and running to the car.

They drove slowly along the runway. Prisoners were being hunted down. An armoured van sped past. Monk waved to the driver. A searchlight fanned across the ground. Sporadic shooting punctuated shouting and screams of pain. A fire had started in the administration building. Black smoke billowed from the windows.

Monk turned the car towards the perimeter fence and the main gates. "There are two sets of gates," he explained. "It's an airlock, a kill zone. Once we're inside we'll be trapped by high fences with no way out." He stopped the car in front of the inner gates. A sentry, cradling a machinegun, emerged from a bunker and moved cautiously towards the vehicle. Others crouched behind sandbags, their weapons aimed at the car.

Monk lowered the driver's window.

"Bloody Hell Monk it's you. What a night!" said the sentry. "Where are you going?"

Monk nodded at his passengers. "I was told to drive them to London."

"To London. What for?"

Monk shrugged. "How should I know? Maybe they've got something special planned for this one." They laughed. The sentry waved to his colleagues. The gates opened and the car moved forward into the airlock. The inner gates swing closed behind them. Floodlights illuminated the road.

A sergeant carrying a pistol and a scanner stepped through a door to their right. "Out of the car." He scanned Monk, checked the name on the screen and nodded. Next was Petch. The scanner beeped. "Do I know you Wilson? There's a Wilson who's a guard here."

"It's not me. I'm from Q division."

"Q division!" The sergeant studied Petch's face. "Where are you taking the prisoner Wilson?"

"To headquarters," answered Petch.

The sergeant scanned Simon and read the display.

"Phillips are you in charge?"

"Yes," answered Simon.

"Why are you taking him to headquarters?"

"To keep him alive. We've been told to get him out of the prison. The others want to kill him, before he talks."

"Wait here. I want to check with the camp commander," said the sergeant and went to a telephone.

"We could grab his gun and hold him hostage. Tell them to open the gate," whispered Monk.

"Yeah and we'd all be dead in five seconds," said Petch.

The sergeant came back. "The phone's dead."

There was a shout, the hammer of a machine gun. Prisoners were running towards the inner gates. A burst of fire. Men fell screaming in pain.

"They're coming for him," said Simon. "Do we go, so you can do your job and stop them?"

The sergeant nodded.

The fugitives moved towards the car.

"Just a minute," said the sergeant. "I haven't finished." He held the scanner against the prisoner's arm and read the display. "Awan Jarwar - you little shit. You're trying to escape aren't you?" He raised the pistol, pressed it against the boy's forehead and cocked it.

The boy was trembling and started to speak. "I not a bomber. These men are..."

"KILL HIM," interrupted Simon. "And we'll never find out who was working with him and you'll be in a cage - in the hanger,"

There was more firing behind them.

The sergeant slowly raised the gun from the boy's face then smashed it down on his skull. Awan Jarwar crumpled.

"Get him out of here," snapped the sergeant. "Open the gates."

The story of eight hundred dangerous terrorists rioting at High Lingham Detention Centre broke on the same morning as the Daily Globe's 'Security Chief Bribery' front page. The riot filled news bulletins and handed competing newspapers alternative headlines.

The director of the OIS chaired a press conference to calm the panic. Hughes was in uniform behind a long table. On each side of him a phalanx of senior officers. James Lucas was at the end of the table away from his boss. "My officers are hunting down these criminals," announced Hughes. "They will all be caught and returned to custody."

"Director Hughes. Have you identified who's being paid by the Americans?"

"Can you tell us the name of the whistleblower?"

An OIS officer leaned across and spoke into Hughes' microphone. "This press conference is to reassure the population that every step necessary is being taken to protect the public during this difficult time. Director Hughes will not be answering questions about the allegation. The matter is being investigated. Next question." He pointed to a journalist at the back of the room.

"How many terrorists have escaped?"

"This is a fluid situation. We don't have an accurate figure yet."

"James, join me for lunch," said Hughes as the press conference ended. "We need to talk."

The OIS director was being unusually civil. They talked as his motorcade sped through London.

"We'll eat at the River Palace. They're expecting us. How are things at Harland?" asked Hughes. "Is John Hume still giving you problems?"

"No director, he seems happy enough."

"I mean is he doing his job properly?"

"Of course. Why do you ask?"

Emlyn Hughes looked at his assistant. "I understood you had a personal issue with him. He was undermining your authority."

"It was a misunderstanding. He's fine."

The limousine crossed Lambeth Bridge overtaking stationery traffic and stopped at the River Palace. Armed OIS men lined the entrance.

"I'm considering moving you back to headquarters. If I do could Hume take over, run Harland. Could he manage Regis?"

"Yes Director, he's capable of taking over," answered Lucas.

The car door opened. "Good. Let's have some lunch."

The maître d' showed them to a private room overlooking the river. Hughes ordered Dover sole with new potatoes and fresh vegetables. "And we'll have a bottle of Montrachet Chardonnay. Relax James. It's a celebration. We can afford a £4,000 bottle of wine. Why not?" The OIS director smiled at his deputy. "One of the benefits of signing my own expenses."

"You don't seem concerned about the riot," said Lucas, "or this business about the bribery allegations."

"Should I be worried?" Hughes looked at his deputy and maintained eye contact. "When you get to my age you learn not to worry about things you can't control. The riot is being dealt with by the camp commander. He's the one who should be worrying... Now the bribery business..." He was still staring at Lucas and smiling.

Lucas looked down at the table.

The food was served as the maître d' opened the wine. "An excellent choice Sir." He sniffed the cork. "It will go well with the fish."

"Are you wondering why I've asked you here."

"It did cross my mind," replied Lucas.

"This financial attack on the OIS, it's a pack of lies of course but the Prime Minister says we must be seen to be clean. No scandal. Do you understand?" He paused. "Would you like my job?"

Lucas put his knife and fork down. "Has he asked you

to resign?"

A mobile phone buzzed. Emlyn Hughes took the phone from his pocket and read a message. "Excuse me. This won't take long." He tapped the keyboard. "I just need to send this. Please, don't let your food get cold."

Lucas put a potato in his mouth and started to chew. He dropped his knife.

The director put his phone away. "What's wrong? You look awful."

"My arm. It's on fire. I can't move it."

"Don't worry. I'm told it doesn't take long." Hughes refilled his glass. "It would be a shame to waste such a good wine." He took a mouthful and savoured it. "You went to the Prime Minister and told him didn't you?"

"How 'id'u 'now?" stammered Lucas.

"He told me." Hughes took another sip. "This really is very good. Did you really think using a mobile phone in a cafe to destroy me would work?"

Lucas' eyes stared at the director but he didn't speak. He couldn't. Dribble and bits of potato ran down his chin.

"Not enjoying your food? We tracked your microchip to the cafe where the phone was used. Coffee and Ginger cake - did you know it's a German tradition, afternoon 'kaffee und kuchen' they call it."

A waiter entered the room.

"Ring for an ambulance," ordered the OIS director. "The deputy director is unwell."

The waiter hurried away.

"You see James I'm not ready to retire just yet and you." He leaned forward. "You're dying so you won't be getting my job after all."

The maître d' arrived with two others. "An ambulance is on its way."

Lucas mumbled something incoherent. He saw the concerned faces but didn't understand what was happening or why it was getting dark.

"He's dead," said the paramedic. "Looks like a stroke."

CHAPTER 21

High Lingham's Camp Commander reported to Hughes by phone. "We've accounted for most of the prisoners. Six hundred and thirty seven re-captured, ninety six dead, forty four wounded and five we haven't found yet."

"What were our casualties?"

"Sixteen dead and five wounded, one shot in the gut. He's not expected to live."

"What are you doing about recapturing the other five prisoners?"

"The outer perimeter wasn't compromised I believe four of them are still somewhere in the prison grounds. It's only a matter of time and we will find them."

Emlyn Hughes made a note of the numbers. "You said five. Now it's four! Which is it, commander?"

"One prisoner got away."

"You said the perimeter wasn't compromised. How did he get away?"

The camp commander hesitated. "Prison guards drove him through the main gate."

"WHAT!" The OIS director was on his feet. "Where was your security?" he shouted. "The cameras, facial recognition, HAVE YOU IDENTIFIED THEM?"

"The control room was on fire. The cameras failed during the riot but we know the men who helped the prisoner escape were scanned as they left. There are three of them, two guards Wilson and Monk and a sergeant named Phillips."

"And the escaped prisoner. Who was he?"

"A lowlife called Jarwar. Not much of a threat. I can't understand why they helped him escape. Phillips in particular. He was a good man."

"They're all traitors. Commander, message me with the IDs of those men and the prisoner's." ordered Hughes. "I'll deal with them. Do it now."

Details of the fugitives appeared on Hughes' computer screen. He opened a new window, typed in a password, pasted the identification numbers into a box and pressed return. The computer asked for a verification code and, when it was entered, accepted the command.

The fugitives were travelling along a back road near Monmouth. Awan Jarwar was the first to react. "Something's wrong with my arm. It feels 'ike 'is on fire." The words were slurred.

"You took a nasty bang on the head last night," said Simon. There was something else. Jarwar's face had dropped on one side. "Can you lift your arms?"

The boy's eyes were wide. He looked terrified. His arms didn't move. His lips moved but no words came.

Monk stopped the car. The boy was drooling. Saliva ran down his chin onto his chest.

"What the fuck's happening to him?" said Petch.

Simon felt a stinging sensation as if a red hot needle had pierced his arm. He tore of his jacket, clawed at the bandage and unwound it, tossing his microchip to the floor. Petch did the same. Monk began to moan, his face was twisted. He tried to speak, to beg for help, to be released from the searing pain in his arm but there was no help for Monk or the boy.

"The microchips," muttered Simon. "So that's why there had to be two way communication."

"What are you talking about?" said Petch.

"It was part of the specification." Simon closed Awan Jarwar's eyes. "I didn't understand why at the time. Don't you see? There must be a trigger to release some kind of nerve agent. It would only take a tiny amount. My God. The entire population's walking around with a poisonous bomb inside them and someone has a switch to trigger it on a whim."

They sat in the car for several minutes. "What now?" asked Petch.

"We need to wash our arms."

They dragged Monk and Jarwar from the car.

"We can't just leave them here, at the side of the road," said Simon. It's not right."

"They're dead. They don't care," said Petch and rolled the bodies into the ditch. They landed face down in the muddy water. "That'll give us a bit more time. I'll drive."

Petch drove to a convenience store where they bought a first aid kit and bottled water. They stopped in a lay-by to wash their arms.

"Do you think they're looking for us?"

"No," replied Petch. "We're dead. They will have found our burnt bodies and microchips where we left them."

Simon wasn't so sure. "What if they DNA test the bodies?"

Sandra Tate was unloading shopping when a car with OIS markings came along the road. She watched it come closer, slowly, menacingly. A knot formed in her stomach. Two men were inside; the driver, a thug of a man and a passenger. She relaxed and tried to understand. The passenger was Simon Reece but he was in uniform.

Simon got out of the car and spoke quietly to her.

He went back to the vehicle. "There's a barn behind the house. Sandra's gone to open it. Put the car in there."

Simon told their story as they ate in the kitchen. Petch said very little, nodding occasionally and adding an odd word. Sandra struggled to comprehend the jumble of things Simon was saying. He seemed hyper, wired, jumping from one thing to another; steel cages, cattle prods, the riot, cutting up corpses, the escape, how Monk and some kid died in the car. She just couldn't accept the chip in her body could kill her. Slowly, as she sorted the pieces, the truth emerged and she understood the horror of it all.

"What are you going to do?" she asked.

"We need to hide," said Simon. "We can't go out. We're not chipped. Thank God we weren't stopped on our way here." He looked at Sandra. "Can we stay?"

She nodded. "I'll get you some clothes tomorrow. We'll burn the uniforms." She nudged Simon and pointed at Petch. His eyes were shut.

"We haven't slept for two days. Thanks Sandra. It's only until I can think of something. We can't stay forever."

"I spoke to Gary Bridger yesterday," said Sandra. "The chief constable told him to re-investigate your fire. He's sent the coat for DNA testing."

"I'd forgotten about the fire. I don't really care. Doesn't seem important anymore."

CHAPTER 22

"The Leader of the Opposition," shouted Mr. Speaker.

Colin Walters, newly appointed Labour Party leader, stood up. His first Prime Minister's question time had to be good. He paused for a moment looking around the chamber. The house was packed. "Following the revelation in the Globe newspaper that a senior security chief has been bribed millions of pounds by the Americans and has compromised our national security, can I ask the Prime Minister why there have been no arrests?"

"Prime Minister."

Max Roberts stood, leaned on the dispatch box and sneered at Walters. "The Right Honourable Gentleman is perfectly aware that no name was given by the Globe. Furthermore, the claims made anonymously are unproven. I believe they were a deliberate attempt to discredit the excellent work the Office of Internal Security is doing in protecting our people. I've asked Director Hughes to investigate the allegations and will report back to the house when we know the facts."

"Leader of the Opposition."

"I thank the Prime Minister for his reply and am pleased the matter is being properly investigated. I'm sure he agrees, the truth must be exposed."

Shouts of, "Hear, hear," echoed around the chamber.

"And... I want to help expose the truth. I ask the Prime Minister, is he aware of the name of the owner of the Cayman Islands bank account which is at the centre of the allegation, the bank account through which three million dollars has passed is EMLYN HUGHES... HIS DIRECTOR OF INTERNAL SECURITY?"

The house erupted with noise. Members leapt to their feet, shouting - demanding a response from the Prime Minister.

"Order, order, order," cried the Speaker.

Roberts thumbed through his briefing notes, searching, in vain, for an answer. He waited until the noise subsided.

Les Romney watched from the public gallery. The Labour leader had used parliamentary privilege and exposed Hughes. Romney had his story. Hughes' name was in the public domain and could now be used in the paper. The spread Romney had already drafted would be published in tomorrow's Globe. It was a great scoop, a 'Journalism of the Year Scoop' - as good as Woodward and Bernstein's Watergate exposé which finished President Nixon - no. This was better. This was Romney's scoop.

"Order," shouted the Speaker. "Prime Minister."

"It's a pity the Right Honourable Gentleman hides behind parliamentary privilege to make a scurrilous accusation. My government is committed to defending the people from attack and Director Hughes is in the vanguard of our defences. Director Hughes is a valued servant to the people. If the Right Honourable Gentleman has ANY evidence he should pass it to the relevant authority for proper investigation."

"There now follows a statement from the Secretary of State for Industry," shouted the Speaker.

The chamber started to empty. PM's question time was over.

Roberts phoned Emlyn Hughes as he was being driven back to Downing Street. "I told you to watch the little shit, You should have finished him straight away. Taken him off at the fucking neck."

Hughes held the phone away from his ear. "I know that now. Max, how was I to know he would tell a newspaper?"

"You're head of security. It's your job to know... Emlyn, clean it up and fast."

"I've already started," said Hughes. "Lucas is history."

"Good. Now sort the rest of the mess you've created."

An OIS snatch squad raided The Globe newspaper offices the following day, too late to stop Les Romney's centre spread. Hughes knew he was in the spotlight. He had to be careful. The editorial staff and the journalist Romney were taken into custody and the paper closed.

News that Romney was a liar who makes up stories quickly spread. His reports from the past were dissected to show how dishonest he was. Evidence appeared showing the Cayman account was faked and Romney was charged with contempt for refusing to reveal his source for the story.

Of course, Hughes knew James Lucas was the source and he also knew how Romney had received to story - anonymously. Romney couldn't reveal who his source was, he didn't know the source.

A date was set for Romney's trial. It was to be the final public destruction of the journalist's reputation.

A knock at the door startled them. Simon Reece and Petch hurried upstairs. Sandra waited before opening the door. The men had been hiding at Coed Mawr for several days, staying away from the windows, away from prying eyes, not daring to go outside.

"It's alright. You can come down."

They followed Gary Bridger into the lounge. "I've got it, the report," he said. "But it's not all good news. There is viable DNA on the coat."

Gary produced his police computer and opened a Regis DNA enquiry. "There are traces from three people but look at this." He pointed at the screen.

Simon looked at the search result. "There's only one name, Alun Bridger, your father."

"We know my father handled the coat, he said he did, so his DNA would be there. But who are the others? Something isn't right."

"Are you saying the others aren't on the data base?" asked Simon.

"It's obvious, isn't it?" said Sandra. They're probably dead."

Gary closed the programme. "No. I don't think so. I'd swear Hughes' DNA is one of the samples. My father gave the coat to him. He's still alive."

"So why isn't Hughes' name showing up?" asked Simon. What did it mean? He wanted to know but how could he find out hidden away in Wales? And there was something else. Staying in Sandra's house was getting difficult. Already Petch was becoming sullen. They had to get out.

"Gary. Is there any way Petch and I can get hold of microchips?"

"You mean false identities?" The policemen considered the question. "If you were scanned they would have to be of real people that are on the database and you'd need to look like them."

"What about the mortuary or an undertaker's?" asked Petch.

Simon remembered the corpses at the airfield. "No. The registrar records all deaths on Regis."

"Easy then," said Petch. "A couple of deaths the registrar isn't told about. We could pick people with the right appearance."

"Seriously? Murder two men and impersonate them?" Simon shuddered. "Gary, you said they have to be real people Regis can identify. But do they? What if we created two new identities on Regis... two fake characters, avatars if you like." Even as he suggested it the idea sounded ridiculous; they had no way of getting to Regis.

The evening news bulletin carried a special item. A statement by Labour leader, Colin Walters. He looked tired and nervous as he read the prepared notes. "I am satisfied the OIS have conducted a thorough investigation into the Cayman allegations. I have now had the opportunity to examine all the evidence and agree with their findings." He paused and wiped his forehead. "Romney and his accomplices at The Globe fabricated the story for their own purposes. I know now it was Romney who sent me the forged documents, knowing I would use Parliamentary Privilege to falsely accuse Director Hughes and put his name in the public arena. I made a foolish and unforgivable mistake for which I am truly sorry. I have written to Director Hughes offering an unreserved apology and state unequivocally here and now that Director Hughes is an honourable man with no stain on his character."

"Bullshit! Look at him. He's been got at," said Simon. "I wonder what they did to him. He's terrified."

"What do you make of this Romney business?" asked Sandra.

"I believe Romney's story. They'll have a show trial and that's the last we'll hear of him."

Simon had trouble sleeping that night. He felt trapped, with no means of escape. Petch was snoring loudly. He had to get out, out of the bedroom, away from Petch, out of the house. Was Regis the key that would solve the puzzle? He didn't know. Would it give him his life back - end the nightmare? Dare he risk everything and contact John Hume?

He got up, dressed quietly and crept downstairs. Sandra's mobile phone was on the kitchen table. He picked it up and slipped out of the back door.

It was still dark when Joy Spencer's phone rang. "Joy. It's Simon."

"Simon who?"

"Me. Simon Reece."

"Is this a joke? If it is it's in very poor taste."

"No Joy. It's not a joke. It really is me."

She switched the bedside light on. "Tell me the name of Mr. Johal's son."

"His son! He didn't have a son. He had three daughters."

"They said you died."

"I nearly did... Joy I need your help."

CHAPTER 23

Joy parked in the lay-by and waited. It was a desolate place miles from anywhere. She'd left Warwick at eight o'clock and was early. A Land Rover emerged from a field. A dog was barking in the back. A small man wearing a flat cap got out and shut the gate. He drove along the road leaving clods of red mud as he went. Minutes passed, then an hour. Simon was late.

"I must be mad." Joy started her engine. "What am I doing here? He isn't coming." She wanted to drive straight back to Warwick and safety. A police car cruised past. The policeman was staring. It went as far as a side road. "Damn. It's coming back." The car slowed and stopped.

The policeman got out and approached. "Step out of the car."

Joy undid her seatbelt and got out. He verified her identity with his scanner. "You're a long way from home. What are you doing in Wales?"

"I'm visiting a friend of mine in Milford Haven. She's not been well."

"Come with me please." The policeman gripped her arm and guided her to the squad car.

"What are you doing? What's this about?"

He opened the back door. "Get in."

Joy tried to argue. To tell him she'd done nothing. He lowered her head and pushed her in.

"Hello Joy," said Simon. "Good to see you. Don't worry. He's a friend."

"I don't understand. What's going on? Why did they say you're dead?"

"There's a lot to tell," said Simon. "Did you mention to anyone you'd spoken me or we were meeting?"

"No, but they'll know. Regis will be tracking both of us."

"Believing that, you took a big risk coming here. Thank you for trusting me." Simon smiled reassuringly. "You will find what I have to say incredible but I promise you it's all true." He went on to tell her almost everything, about the prison escape, the deaths of Monk and the young Asian boy from Luton. "Do you understand Joy? The chip inside you can kill you."

Joy sat looking at the policeman standing outside the car. "Who's he?" A black SUV appeared in the distance. It was coming towards them.

"He's a friend," said Simon and slid down in his seat.

"What are you doing?"

"They mustn't see me."

The vehicle slowed and stopped. The passenger window opened. The policemen was saying something to the men in the SUV. He laughed, waved, walked back to the car and opened the door.

"What's happening Gary?" asked Simon.

"They're OIS," whispered the policeman. "Joy, I've told them I stopped you for a breath test. They've scanned you and want to check your identity. You need to get out. Keep down Simon. They don't know there's another person in the car."

Gary Bridger led Joy to the SUV where she stood while her face was compared with her Regis computer screen image. The SUV drove away.

"It's OK. They've gone," said Gary Bridger opening the car door. "Thank God, the lazy sods didn't get out and have a look."

Joy tried to light a cigarette. She fumbled and threw it on the ground. "I don't understand. They must have known you were in the car."

Simon shook his head. "I told you, the chip can kill you."

"You mean you haven't got one?.. You said you wanted me to do something." She glared at Simon. "What is it?"

"I need you to talk to John Hume, to ask for his help. I know it's risky but there's no other way. This is what you need to tell him..." Simon explained what he wanted her to say.

"Where are you staying?" she asked. "How do I contact you?"

"The mobile number I rang you from. You'll have it in your phone. Use that, and Joy... Be careful how you talk to John. He might not be willing to help."

"Be careful! Being careful won't help if he turns me in. I've got to go. My friend's expecting me, remember, in Milford Haven."

Simon had told Joy everything, trusting her to approach John Hume and beg for help. He knew the risks. Joy could go to the OIS tell them he was alive. Hume could betray them. Even now, Joy might be in an OIS detention camp, in a cage, like Simon was. They could use her to trap him.

"You're a fool," said Petch. "She'll lead them straight here. You used Sandra's phone. The signal, they'll know where we are."

Simon didn't answer.

"Maybe she won't ring. She won't ask Hume for help. Probably decided she's safer if you stay dead, tells no one and gets on with her life."

"Shut up Petch," snapped Simon. He got up and went to the door.

"Where are you going?"

"Out. I need some air."

Sandra found Simon on the beach. "You shouldn't be here. It's not safe."

"I know. Nothing's safe anymore. Is it really worth it?"

"It's Petch, isn't it?"

Simon sat down on the hull of an upturned dingy. "He snores like a pig, is constantly complaining. It's driving me mad."

"He's trapped as well," said Sandra. "He's a fighter. He's bored."

"We sat here once before, that afternoon. Do you remember?"

Sandra joined him and sat on the boat. "Yes. It was sunny. Like today..."

They watched a family playing football. The man gently tapped the ball towards his young daughter. An older boy ran and kicked it away from her. The breeze carried the ball down the beach.

"That wasn't nice, Jason," shouted the man. "Quick, get the ball before it goes in the sea."

The girl started to cry.

"She rang," said Sandra and handed Simon the phone.

"What did she say?"

"Nothing. She asked for you and hung up. Call her back."

Simon toyed with the phone. "What do you think? Did she sound nervous?"

"Yes... Simon, you've started this. You knew what might happen. You can't hide forever. Ring her."

He called Joy Spencer. "Joy? It's Simon. What did he say?"

"He didn't believe me at first. Said I was lying, it was impossible - that the chips are passive and can't hurt anyone... He was angry. I thought he was going to report me."

"I'm sorry Joy, for involving you."

"This morning a small cardboard box was delivered to my flat. Later the phone rang. It was John. He told me not to open the box, to give it to you. Said, you'll know what to do with it. He wants to see you."

Joy drove to Wales the following day. Simon was waiting in the lay-by they'd used before.

She handed Simon the box. "He said not to look inside until you're secure. The instructions are in the box. What did he mean?"

"He means where there are no scanners, no cameras or prying eyes."

"So he's done it. Sent what you wanted."

"Or a bomb."

"A bomb!" said Joy. "Oh God! Do you really think so?"

"I hope not but these are dangerous times." Simon pushed the box into his pocket. "Go home Joy. None of this ever happened. We never met. It's too dangerous. I don't want you involved anymore."

She leaned over and kissed his cheek. "Take care, Simon."

Sandra and Petch were in the kitchen when Simon got back to Coed Mawr. He produced the box and slit it open with a knife revealing a foil envelope containing a flash-drive and two microchips. They plugged the flash-drive into Sandra's laptop.

"Damn! It's encrypted," said Simon. "It won't open without the key."

"Is this what you need?" Sandra showed him a text on her phone. "It's gibberish. I nearly deleted it." They copied the encryption key into the computer.

The drive opened. Two men's profiles appeared.

"That's my picture. He's sent our Regis files," said Petch. "He's playing with us. It's a bloody joke!"

"No," said Simon. "Look at the names. He's used our images - created two new identities."

Simon Reece was now self employed plasterer, Jim Parson, from Cambridge and Petch a plumber named Tony Walsh.

"What about the microchips? Do we implant them?" asked Petch.

"No way," said Simon. "We'll wrap them in plastic and tape them in place. As long as our arms are covered no one will know." He opened a notepad file on the flash drive and read the contents.

"Simon, the two identities, I've created, will go live on Regis at 6 o'clock this evening. Keep the microchips shielded until then and don't get stopped or scanned before they are activated. Meet me at The Prince Regent pub in Regent Street, Cambridge at 11am tomorrow."

"Can I use your car?" asked Simon.

Sandra nodded.

"I'll leave early."

"I need a change," said Petch. "I'm coming with you."

CHAPTER 24

The two men turned on to the M5 and headed north. Simon checked his watch. Seven o'clock. "We've made good time. If the M42 isn't jammed we'll be early."

"I need a piss," said Petch. "There's a service area up ahead."

"Are you sure? There'll be cameras, automatic scanning in the entrance."

"We have to test these sometime." Petch patted his arm. "Or should we keep going and I'll piss out of the window?"

They pulled into Strensham services and drove around looking for a space.

Simon pointed to an OIS car parked by the entrance. "Do you still want a piss?"

A coach pulled up next to the OIS car. Elderly people, some with walking aids, started to disembark and move towards the building. Petch got out of the car, pushed his way through the old people and disappeared inside. Simon sat and watched the coach party negotiate their way slowly through the doors. A woman with a walking frame stumbled and fell in the doorway. A crowd gathered around her.

Two OIS officers appeared and helped her to her feet. They strolled to their car, un-shouldered their weapons, got in and drove away. Simon followed Petch into the services and headed, past the shops and fast food outlets, towards the toilets.

Petch was coming the other way, carrying two cups of coffee. "Easy. I looked straight at the security cameras. Nothing!"

"I saw the OIS men come out. They weren't in a hurry. I guessed you were OK."

"One stood next to me at the urinal." Petch grinned. "I spoke to him."

John Hume was in the bar at the back of the Prince Regent when they arrived. Simon went in first, bought a drink and joined him at a table.

"How are you Simon?" asked Hume. "It's been a while."

Simon sat down. "You look tired John... How are things at Harland?"

The door opened. Petch came in and sat on a bar stool. "A pint of IPA and a double whisky."

"So you brought Mr. Walsh with you." Hume leaned forward and spoke quietly. "Be careful Simon, Petch is a killer."

"Thanks for the new identities. Using our own images, that was clever."

"I didn't believe Joy at first when she said there was poison in the chips. It sounded like fantasy, a ridiculous film plot."

"What changed your mind John? Made you want to help?"

John Hume drew a small circle in condensation on the table. "After Joy told me, I started to wonder. I remembered how James Lucas' died. I opened his Regis database and there he was."

"You said, there he was. I don't understand. What was

in his database?"

"Hughes, Emlyn Hughes was logged into Lucas' record the minute before he had his stroke. Why would he be doing that while they were having lunch together?" Hume sponged the condensation with a beer mat. "The day before, Hughes rang me, asked if I could run Harland without Lucas. I hated Lucas. The man was a snake. I said yes - of course. I'd love to."

"It might just have been a coincidence," said Simon.

"No. It wasn't a coincidence. I got two of my guys, ones I could trust, to reverse engineer all the links the OIS have made to Regis. Nothing worked. They couldn't work out how it happened. It didn't make any sense so they started with a chip and worked back, spoofing links, until they found a trigger in the chip which accepted the termination command. Regis is just the identifier. The command comes from a programme at OIS. The victim's chip leaks a molecule of nerve agent and that's it." He clicked his fingers. "Simon, it's not just Lucas. They've murdered hundreds of people."

"Do you remember when we were going to sell Harland and the Americans came over? asked Simon. "That time, in Madingley Hall, after the man was stabbed by the river? I said, 'The new laws Roberts wanted would protect the people. They made a lot of sense.' Do you remember?"

Hume shook his head. "I remember the stabbing."

"John, you said, 'It was Orwellian madness. Roberts was a fascist. Britain would be a police state.' You were more right than either of us could ever guess. I was a.."

Movement by the door distracted Simon. Two OIS men were standing there. "This is a routine check," said one. They moved around the room scanning customers, checking identities. "Name," demanded the officer.

Simon stood up. "Parson, Jim Parson."

The OIS man looked at his screen. "You're a plasterer. What are you doing here, Parson?"

"He was offering to do some work at my house," said John Hume. "I'm having a new kitchen fitted."

The scanner swept along Hume's arm. 'John Hume, - CLASSIFIED,' appeared in the display.

"I'm sorry Mr. Hume," said the OIS man. "I didn't know."

"You didn't ask," said Hume. "That man by the bar is waiting to speak to me." He pointed at Petch. "He's a plumber, name of Walsh. Now, I need to finish with these men and get back to my office. Director Hughes is expecting me to call this afternoon and I don't want keep him waiting."

The OIS officer stepped back and glanced nervously at his colleague. "Let's go. We're done here."

"He was frightened of you," said Simon. "Couldn't get away fast enough. Why?"

"Simon, you don't know? It was what he saw on the scanner - Classified."

"I don't remember anything classified in Regis. What does it mean?"

"It means my data is restricted. He can't access anything about me. It's an OIS addition to Regis. Was made after you were sacked." Hume looked at his watch and stood up. "I've got to go. Simon, you've got your new identity. Go and live Jim Parson's life somewhere quiet."

"John, we can't just ignore what's happening. Put our heads in the sand!"

"Don't you understand, Simon? Hughes can't be stopped. He's a serial killer protected by the Prime Minister. The state security services are at his disposal. At the click of a mouse, on a whim, he can kill any of us. Damn right I'm going to keep my head in the sand."

"... Is Hughes' Classified?" asked Simon.

"Of course. He ordered us to create the classified list. Why?"

"So a Regis DNA search won't show him up?"

"Not unless the searcher has access to the classified

file."

So that was it; why Hughes' DNA could have been on the coat but didn't register when Gary Bridger did his search. "John I need your help one last time and then, I promise, I won't bother you again."

Hume sat down again. "Don't push it. I don't owe you anything. I've already risked my neck for you," he whispered.

The barman came over and picked up their glasses. "You finished with these?"

"Yes," snapped Hume.

Petch turned and looked at Hume.

"I know, you took a chance and I'm grateful," said Simon. "But it's important. You have access to the classified files. I need you to check something for me; DNA samples. I think one may belong to Hughes. I think he was involved in the murder of my parents."

"Your parents? You're mad. What good would it do if he was? He's untouchable."

"Please John. You've come this far. Believe me, there's no other way."

The Prime Minister was in good humour. He made some notes on the draft of his speech, initialled the paper with a flourish and returned it to his aide. It was time to tell the world, the fight against terrorism was almost won. He, Max Roberts, had delivered what he'd promised. "I want it to be a big rally, packed with NPP members."

"Preparations are well advanced Prime Minister. The hall has 900 seats. Invitations have been sent out."

"Good, and television coverage?"

"All channels will be broadcasting your speech live."

"Excellent. The footage of the arrests looks good. We'll use the clips to illustrate our success. Make sure they're distributed to the news channels but embargoed until the day of the rally. Get Director Hughes on the phone."

The aide withdrew. A telephone rang on Roberts' desk.

"Emlyn, I've read your report. Not a single terrorist attack in the last month. Well done. However, we need to be careful. We need to improve OIS's image. Show the people you're the good guys. I want you at the rally, on stage with me. I'm going to congratulate my security chief publicly."

"You don't need me there to do that Max. Just say something in your speech. I'd prefer to stay in the background."

"This isn't a discussion. You're going to be there... Relax Emlyn. You'll be fine. Another thing, after the rally I'm flying to the States. The President has invited me and you're coming with me. He loves Regis, what we've achieved, and wants to learn more."

CHAPTER 25

Despite being afraid, John Hume agreed to help Simon. He'd told Simon he could access the classified files but he knew any attempt to log in using his own administrator permissions and search the data would be seen. John Hume poking around searching for something would be flagged by the OIS. There had to be another way in, a way that was anonymous, untraceable. Was the answer to hack into Regis as an outsider just as Systron had done when they wanted to buy Harland Digital? But how? Systron had used a Neutrino Exploit Kit to get in but that wouldn't work. Regis had been upgraded, with extra defences; firewalls strengthened to block any hacker's attack.

There had to be another way. The attack would have to be from within the firewalls but done in such a way it would go undiscovered. Getting to the file and searching could be done using someone else's login and password. That was it. Hume would use his admin access to steal an OIS operative's identity and use it to log in using a series of proxy servers. Even then, he knew, if he tried to exfiltrate data the system would alarm. It was programmed to guard against data theft by anyone including staff. Unless, that is, he could make the firewall momentarily fail.

Hume identified a clerical officer in OIS headquarters who wasn't at his desk as a suitable victim, and went to work. Soon he was in the classified executive files.

'Two DNA matches,' said the computer screen. John Hume opened the first link. A picture of OIS Director, Emlyn Hughes appeared. Simon Reece was right. Hughes' DNA was on the coat. Hume clicked the second file and gasped. He pressed the download button and waited. 'Fifty six seconds,' said the timer. 'Forty seconds.' The green bar was hardly moving. 'Thirty-five seconds.' A download icon appeared in the corner of the screen. 'Twenty-five seconds.' Hume grabbed it and dropped it into the flash drive. 'Eleven seconds.' "Come on, come on." 'Five, four, three, two, one.' There it was. He grabbed the second file and moved it to the flash drive. The screen froze then turned black. Bile rose up from Hume's stomach. He was scared. The firewall had triggered. They knew. He had to tell Simon. To warn him they were in danger.

Cyber security officer Heath hurried up the last flight of stairs, through the doors to the executive suite and into reception. He took out a handkerchief, wiped his face and waited.

The receptionist pointed to a chair. "He's on the phone." Heath didn't sit.

A voice shouted from the director's office. "I don't care how many men it takes. Do it."

A light flashed on the receptionist's phone. "Is Heath here?"

"Yes Director."

"Send him in."

It was Heath's first and, he believed, about to be his last visit to the citadel on the top floor of OIS headquarters.

Director Hughes was at his desk. "Well? You said it was important."

Heath had rehearsed the scene in his mind. This wasn't

going to be easy. "We detected a cyber attack on Regis."

"Have you dealt with it?"

"Yes Sir. We locked the hackers out."

Hughes signed a paper on his desk. "You detected a hack and blocked it." He looked up. "Why are you wasting my time?"

"Whoever it was accessed classified documents." Heath waited for the explosion.

"What did they look at?" demanded Hughes.

"It was a general sweep. A DNA search enquiry in the classified executive database."

"What?" Hughes focussed on the young computer programmer standing in front of his desk. "I was told that data was totally secure. You... You promised there was no way it could be got at."

"There's something else Sir. We believe some files were copied and downloaded. We don't know who the hackers were. The attackers infiltrated through proxy servers. We're still investigat..."

"FIND THEM," ordered Director Hughes. "GO ON... GET OUT."

Chief Constable Kidger looked at his visitors; Constable Bridger and a man claiming he was Simon Reece but identified by his microchip as Jim Parson. "It's unbelievable. The whole thing," said Kidger.

"Don't you see?" asked Simon. "It means he was there. He killed my parents."

"How did you get this?" Kidger held up the flash drive.

"A friend got it for me. Isn't it enough evidence? What more do you need?"

Kidger stroked his chin. "When I said investigate the case I never expected this. I believe you're Simon Reece and are involved in some strange affair but the rest - it's so far fetched... Is this the only copy of the files?"

"No. There are a number of copies."

"I thought there would be." The Chief Constable got

up and stood with his back to them. "I'll be keeping this copy. I want to think about what you have told me."

After Simon and Gary had gone the Chief Constable called a friend he'd attended police college with; Matthew Broad, Metropolitan Police Commissioner. "Hi Matt. Listen. A case we're investigating has thrown up an unidentified DNA and I need some advice. I want to ask you about Regis. Is there a second database, a secret one containing details of the great and the good?"

"A secret database! That's an odd question," said Broad. "Not that I know of. Why?"

"Come on Matt. It's me... Vince. You're well connected. Can't you..."

"Sorry. I have no idea what you are talking about." The line went dead.

Matthew Broad rang back minutes later. "Vince, you need to be careful. My office phone calls are being recorded. Things have happened... I know the OIS listen in. That bastard Hughes is all over the Met. like a rash."

"So there is a secret database."

"Yes. The OIS executive files are restricted access. Even I'm not supposed to know about them and I'm the most senior policeman in the country. What's this about?"

"Not on the phone," said Kidger. "We need to meet."

A black people carrier overtook John Hume and slowed to a stop. Another boxed him in from behind. Combat clad men dragged him from his car, snapped cable ties on his wrists, hooded him and bundled him away. Heath had followed the breadcrumb trail back to the hacker. No one spoke as they drove. Hume had no idea where he was being taken. He was pulled from the car and manhandled down flights of stairs. A heavy door slammed somewhere nearby, echoing through a building. Hume was forced down onto a chair. He could smell cigarette smoke.

"Do you know where you are?" asked a voice.

Hume shook his head. Strong hands pulled the hood

off. He was in a dirty white tiled room. He blinked. A fluorescent light flickered lazily above him. Beside Hume stood a large man wearing a white shirt, perfectly creased suit trousers, a tie and red braces. He was holding the hood. Opposite Hume sat two men. An older man with greasy black hair and OIS Director Emlyn Hughes.

The older man was smoking. "What did you do with the files you stole?"

Hume shook his head.

"We aren't playing games Mr. Hume. I'll ask you once more. "What did you do with the files you uploaded?"

A fist connected with the side of Hume's head knocking him to the floor. He landed on his face at Hughes' feet. Crack, a polished shoe crushed his hand, breaking bones. He cried out.

They pulled him up, back on the chair. Squinting, he saw Hughes sitting, legs crossed, composed, watching.

The older man asked again. "What did you do with the files you copied?"

Hume didn't answer.

The beating continued. His right ear exploded in pain.

"...I gave them to someone."

"Who?" demanded Hughes. He moved towards Hume and whispered. "Tell me and the pain will end."

"Simon Reece."

"You're a liar," spat Hughes. "Reece is dead. We found his burnt body at High Lingham."

"Yes," mumbled Hume. "Reece is dead."

They hit again and again until he passed out.

The door opened. "Director, you need to go - the rally," said an aide.

Hughes looked at his watch and turned to the older man. "When he comes round. Question him again. I want the truth."

The conference hall was filling as Hughes arrived. A crowd spilled onto the road and was pushed back by OIS officers.

Television crews filmed. Reporters said their packages to camera, adding to the buzz of excitement - the party like anticipation.

In Llangranog, as elsewhere, the Ship Inn was crowded with drinkers intently watching the big screen. Alun Bridger had arrived early and was seated at the bar.

Sandra joined him. "Has it started?"

"Not yet. Hatchet Hughes has just arrived," said Alun. "Look at him. Thinks he's Cock of the Roost."

Bodyguards escorted Hughes through the atrium, past queues waiting to be security screened. He joined the Prime Minister in the green room behind the stage. Roberts was sat on a high stool. A make-up artist was styling his hair. She sprayed it and removed the plastic cape protecting his suit.

"You're late," said the Prime Minister. He got up, walked to the drinks table and poured a whisky. "Want one?" Hughes shook his head.

A technician appeared in the doorway. "Twenty minutes Prime Minister."

Hughes' phone buzzed. He looked at the screen. "Hume dead. Didn't talk." The OIS director slipped the phone into his pocket.

Laughter came from the auditorium; the warm-up act was priming the audience, working them up - ready to greet the Prime Minister. Helpers handed out flags and banners. Coloured spotlights fanned across the seats.

"Ten minutes Prime Minister."

"We need a mighty roar when Max Roberts comes out. The world will be watching," shouted the warm-up. "Let's try one now."

The audience cheered, clapped and whistled in mock approval.

"Come on. We can do better than that. Pretend you've won twenty million on the lottery. Again and put your hearts into it."

"One minute Prime Minister."

The Prime Minister drained his glass. "Is everything ready?" He grinned.

"We have the White House on the line," said an aide. "The President is standing by."

Max Roberts walked from the green room.

"Ladies and gentlemen," said the warm-up. "It's my great pleasure to welcome the man who guided the fight against terrorism, who had the moral courage to do what was needed at a dangerous time, who took on the liberal elite to protect the people. Please give a big welcome to Prime Minister, Max Roberts."

The audience leapt to its feet, clapping and cheering. Roberts acknowledged the applause and waited for the noise to subside. He raised his hands motioning for quiet.

"Thank you... The week I took office there were riots. We all remember them. The burnt-out buildings, the looting, the bombing of fine public servants like Emily Sharp and her entire family - her two young children and the shootings."

A man coughed somewhere in the audience.

"I promised when I became Prime Minister we would stop the riots, we would stop the looting and the bombings. There have been complainers who've said we were too harsh, that microchips were an infringement of liberty, that... the cost was too high. Was it?" Roberts scanned the audience. "Let me remind you what we were fighting."

The lights dimmed. A film started to play. Whitechapel Road, hundreds of protestors, a youth trying to throw a petrol bomb, igniting himself in a ball of flame, the bodies of men, women and children after the bombing at Mardenheath American Air Force Base, arrests, the burnt out wreckage of Emily Sharps car, a charred child's toy on the pavement, a prison van bringing Masood Khan to court. There were boos and angry shouts from the audience and gasps as graphic pictures of the riot at High Lingham appeared on the screen. The film ended.

"Sobering isn't it?... And it wasn't just here. Our friends and allies in America have been fighting the same war. Taking on the terrorists."

The US President appeared on the screen. "Your Prime Minister, Max Roberts, has done a great job beating down on the bad guys. Great job. I know him personally. I've known him for many years. He's a good man. He's been a good friend to America. The wicked, evil men, really evil men you've been fighting, like we have here, have killed women and children. . . Little babies, imagine, killing a little baby! I told the Prime Minister, 'The only way to beat the terrorists is to get tough, take difficult decisions.' I told him what to do and he listened. He learnt from us. He's not dumb. Max, well done. I look forward to your visit next month."

"Thank you Mr. President and I do too." The screen faded to muted applause. "Now you've seen what we were fighting and now I would like to introduce the man who led our campaign, the man who did the heavy lifting. I'm talking about Director Hughes who envisaged and then created the Office of Internal Security."

Hughes joined Roberts on stage and stepped up to the podium. "Thank you Prime Minister. When you asked me to propose a way of taking on the terror in our midst I confess it was a daunting challenge" He looked past the autocue to a face in the front row, the face of Simon Reece, the face of a dead man!

Hughes swallowed. "When you tasked me with creating the Office of Internal Security I was proud to have the opportunity to serve my country."

Hughes noticed police officers moving through the audience. He sipped a mouthful of water. The glass slipped from the lectern and shattered on the floor. He looked again. The front row seat was empty.

A noise off-stage distracted Hughes. He turned and looked. Policemen were disarming his bodyguards. Behind them, the Prime Minister was being shepherded away by security men. The audience watched, waiting for Hughes to say something to continue his speech. Millions of viewers held their breath.

Hughes turned back towards the audience and saw loathing and disgust in a sea of faces. He focussed on the autocue searching desperately for the next line. "... More than three thousand criminals..." The autocue went blank. Hughes was alone, vulnerable and afraid.

Simon watched from the side of the stage. "Are you ready for this?"

Gary Bridger was grinning. "Dad'll be enjoying every minute."

Policemen walked onto the stage.

"BREAKING NEWS," flashed across television screens. "OIS Director Emlyn Hughes' arrested for the murders of Aaron Green and James Lucas," ran the ticker line on the bottom of screens.

Customers, watching on The Ship Inn's big screen, cheered as television cameras moved in for a close up of Hughes' ashen face. Alun Bridger hugged Sandra.

"Doesn't look so cocky now does he?" said Sandra. They watched as Hughes was handcuffed and taken from the stage.

The audience whistled and jeered as he disappeared from view.

"The Prime Minister is in the green room," said Gary. "They're waiting for us there."

Simon followed Gary to the back of the stage. Officers scanned them and opened the green room door. The Metropolitan Police Commissioner stood on the far side of the room.

The Prime Minister was sitting on a sofa. "Who the hell are you?"

"Have you got it?" asked the commissioner.

"Yes Sir," replied Gary. "Maxwell Roberts I have a warrant for your arrest."

"My arrest! You prat. Arrest for what?" Roberts leaned

against the back of his seat. "This is a joke, isn't it? I'm the Prime Minister. I have Crown Immunity. You can't arrest me."

"For the murders of Simon Frederick Jackson and Florence Jackson."

"Now I know it's a joke." Roberts laughed. He went to the drinks table, served himself and emptied the glass. "I've never heard of these people. Who are they?"

"My parents," said Simon. "You bastard. You killed them when you fire bombed their house."

"Commissioner, why are you allowing this charade?" Roberts looked at Simon. "I don't know who you are but you're a fool. Do you have evidence to support this allegation?" He stood up and moved towards the door.

Commissioner Broad stepped between the Prime Minister and the door. "No public announcement will be made until a full investigation is completed. You've been overworking and need a rest Prime Minister; a stay at Chequers to recover. My men will escort you." He tapped on the door.

"This is ridiculous. You idiot, get out of my way. I'm going to America."

"No Sir. You are going to Chequers," said the Commissioner firmly. "Your car is waiting."

CHAPTER 26

Hughes' arrest and Max Roberts' disappearance changed the political landscape. The OIS reign of terror was over. The snatch squads were disbanded. Key officers, suspected of grievous crimes, arrested and interrogated. Some tried to escape, to flee the country. An old man with black greasy hair, Hughes' interrogator, was identified by facial recognition at Portsmouth attempting to drive aboard a ferry to Spain. His assistant, the younger man, the man who beat Hume to death, was never found. Cages at High Lingham and other detention centres opened releasing hundreds of innocent prisoners. Others were not so lucky. Computer files at OIS headquarters told the grim story; of the people taken who would never return to their loved ones, of others driven insane by torture. The records were meticulous, detailed and chilling. The horrors perpetrated by the OIS, in the name of state security, were all there, recorded in Regis. Regis the weapon used by the OIS to manipulate, control and brutalise the country identified every evil act, every death, proving guilt, revealing those responsible. Hughes, in particular, exposed as a sadistic monster, a man, who enjoyed killing by remote control, of pressing a button on his computer or phone, poisoning hundreds with a nerve agent already hidden in their bodies.

"But where?" the investigators asked, "was the evidence of Robert's guilt." They searched for it and found nothing. No orders from Roberts, no recording of him telling Hughes to commit the crimes, no witnesses to his involvement. Nothing linked him to the command structure of the Office of Internal Security. Of course, he denied knowing anything, blaming Hughes and then there was the money, the Cayman Island bank account.

"That," said Roberts, "proves Hughes was working alone. That Hughes is also a traitor who deceived the government, who deceived me. I thought he was my friend but all the time he was selling secrets to the Americans and lining his own pocket."

Speculation about Roberts mounted. "Where was he?" demanded the newspapers. No one knew for sure but Roberts was safe secure in, his guarded citadel, Chequers.

Roberts was walking in the gardens, enjoying the early spring flowers, when an unexpected visitor arrived; Sir Jason Langwade, the Attorney General. Langwade, a portly man, grey haired, old before his time with an air of gravitas, was an experienced lawyer on a mission which made him uncomfortable. The sky was clear and blue. The sun was shining but it was a cold morning and Roberts was dressed in an overcoat. The two men strolled to a bench at the end of the formal gardens. They sat down facing towards the house.

"Suddenly it's a small world," said Roberts and pointed to the red brick wall behind them. "This is as far as I'm allowed... Well? What have you got to tell me Langwade?"

"A date has been set for Hughes' trial. He's charged with crimes against humanity."

"So he goes before the International Court of Justice?"

"No," replied Langwade. "He's to be tried at the Old Bailey." The lawyer wiped a dew-drop from his nose. "Why are we sitting in the shade? I'm freezing." He stood up and moved into the sunshine.

"You should have brought a coat."

Langwade blew his nose. "I'm here to tell you that there's no evidence linking you to Hughes' crimes. He's tried to implicate you, swears you gave the orders but there is no proof to support his claims."

"Hughes always was a snake. I never really trusted him but I had no idea how evil he was or what he was doing," said Roberts. "All those poor people. Can you imagine? He should be hanged."

The lawyer took a deep breath and relayed the message he'd been sent with, the one he most disliked. "The decision is, you are not to be charged with any crimes committed by the Office of Internal Security."

Roberts grinned and jumped up. "So that's it. I'm free."

"Not quite. There's still the arson attack at Coed Mawr. Hughes alleges you set the fire and, as you know, there is evidence to support his claim; the DNA on the coat recovered from the crime scene which proves you were there."

Max Roberts turned away and walked along the lawn. He stopped and rubbed the back of his neck. "What happens now?" he shouted from the corner of the garden.

The lawyer projected his voice, "We are going to wait until Hughes's trial is over and then it will be your turn in the dock. You will be prosecuted for arson and the murder of Mr and Mrs Jackson on the 14th September 1980. Until then you will be kept at a secure location."

Robert walked back to the lawyer. "You mean I will continue to be held here a prisoner?"

"Mr. Roberts, you are no longer Prime Minister. Chequers is the Prime Minister's country residence. Those men..." Langwade pointed to suited men on the terrace, "are your new security. They will take you to your new home." The lawyer sniffed and walked back to the house, satisfied he'd delivered his message.

"Hughes trial continues in camera," announced the news anchor.

"Come and listen," shouted Sandra. She turned up the volume as Simon came into the kitchen. The television cut to a presenter outside the Old Bailey.

"Day eleven of the Trial of Director Hughes and a surprise ruling by Judge Damien Foster - to protect national security, evidence is to be heard 'in camera'. Immediately following the judge's direction the public gallery was cleared and reporting restrictions imposed. The trial is expected to last another seven weeks. This is Dave Hawley for the BBC.."

"It's not surprising. What else could they do?" said Simon. "Imagine the panic if people knew the truth."

The image cut back to the studio. "In other news Prime Minister Walters has announced the programme to remove personal microchips will be speeded up." Footage of people queuing outside a clinic appeared. "He says it will be completed before the end of the year."

Sandra turned the television off. "What do you think they've done with Roberts?"

"I've no idea. Since his resignation as Prime Minister he seems to have vanished."

"Do you think he wanted to resign?"

Simon poured a coffee. "No. The reports saying he's ill and suffering from stress are nonsense. I asked the Chief Constable what was going on, why Roberts hadn't been charged with my parents' murder."

"Yes, you told me but surely they've completed the investigation by now. They have the evidence."

"He said the politics were complicated - I needed to be patient."

Max Roberts had watched the same news bulletin. He got up from the sofa, poured a large whisky and went to the window. A gardener was mowing the lawn. Gates, shut and locked, at the end of the gravel drive were guarded by an armed sentry. Roberts placed the glass between the bars on the windowsill. His new home, a large house in its own grounds, was remote - away from public view. He looked at the security camera in the corner of the room and gestured with one finger.

In the kitchen Charlie Benson was preparing Roberts' evening meal. Newly graduated, it was his first job. Charlie enjoyed working at the house and secretly admired Max Roberts.

"Charlie, that was a fantastic fish pie," said Roberts after he'd eaten. "Where did you learn to cook like that?"

Charlie blushed as he cleared the table. "At Birmingham Catering College Mr. Roberts."

"Do you have a car Charlie?" asked Roberts, casually.

"Yes, a clapped out Fiesta."

"That's a shame. A young man as talented as you deserves something better."

Charlie carried the tray to the kitchen, scraped the plates and loaded the dishwasher.

The door opened. "Everything alright Charlie?" asked a guard.

"Yeah. He's eaten. I'm done for the night."

The guard shut the door.

Charlie was putting his coat on when the door opened again. Roberts came into the kitchen. "Are you going home Charlie?" He placed a small piece of paper on the table and nodded at it.

Charlie picked the note up and read, "Is there a camera in the kitchen?" He shook his head.

"Microphone?" mouthed Roberts.

"No, Mr. Roberts."

"Good." Roberts smiled. "Charlie, can I trust you?" He motioned to a chair. "Sit down. I want to ask you something. How would you like to earn a great deal of money?"

"How much are you talking about?"

"Twenty thousand pounds. Enough to buy a decent

car, a new one even."

"Twenty thousand!" Charlie unbuttoned his coat and sat down. "What do you want me to do?"

Roberts leaned forward and spoke quietly. "I want you to buy something for me and bring it to the house...."

The young man listened intently.

"I want you to buy me a chemistry set."

"A chemistry set. What for?"

"It's difficult to explain. It's called a CRISPR Kit. Here I've written down the details." He passed a small piece of paper to Charlie. "You can buy it from one of the big online retailers. That's all you have to do. Twenty thousand pounds Charlie for five minutes effort. Think of it."

"I'm not sure. What about the guards? Won't they say something?"

"How much do you earn a week? Three hundred a week."

Charlie shook his head. "Nothing like."

"And I bet you have to pay tax... You would probably have to work for two years or more to make what I'm offering you."

Driving back to his rented room at the Black Swan Charlie planned how he was going to spend the money. A car, maybe, but before then a holiday in the Caribbean for sure.

He bought a pint of bitter, took it upstairs, locked the bedroom door and turned on his laptop.

Slowly he typed CRISPR–Cas9 making sure it was spelt exactly as Roberts had written. An image appeared on the screen. "DIY Bacterial Genome Engineering CRISPR Kit $169," said the description. "Buy now!" flashed the prompt. Twenty thousand pounds - a new car and a holiday. He shrugged, clicked buy and completed the order.

The next morning Charlie told Robert his chemistry set was one the way.

An innocuous looking box, with a smiley mouth on

one end, arrived two days later.

No one asked what was in the carrier bag when Charlie went to work. "It's hidden in the cupboard under the sink," he whispered as he delivered Roberts' breakfast.

Roberts had a newspaper on the table and was doing a crossword.

Charlie turned his back on the camera in the corner of the room. "Where's my money?" he mouthed.

"What do you think?" asked Roberts. "In a while - Five letters,"

Charlie didn't understand.

"The clue." Roberts pointed at the crossword.

"Later," said Charlie.

"Later - of course. I should have known. Thank you Charlie."

Charlie returned to the kitchen wondering when he was going to get paid.

At three o'clock the following morning Roberts got up. The house was silent. Would they be monitoring the cameras? Roberts didn't know. It was a chance he had to take. He moved quietly down the stairs to the kitchen, carefully closed the door and waited. The box was under the sink just as Charlie had said. The hall clock chimed the hour, then silence. Roberts waited listening for a sound, for footsteps in the hall, a voice but no one came to investigate. He was in luck. No one was watching the security monitors. Roberts opened the box and studied the contents. He read the instructions, unwrapped three small plastic tubes and put them in the freezer. Roberts read the instructions a second time. He pulled on latex gloves, spread newspaper over the kitchen table, unpacked bottles, plates, powders and tubes of E-Coli and arranged them in neat lines. The last item, a miniature centrifuge, was in a blister pack.

He collected the tubes from the freezer, picked up a pipette and counted drops of CRISPR ingredients into them. Next he added the contents of a tiny bottle labelled E-Coli.

Roberts read the instructions again. "Add five drops of Cas9 to the compound." He wanted to hurry - to get the job done before he was discovered but he had to get it right. He shook the tubes and spread the liquid on plastic culture plates.

Roberts covered the plates with plastic film. He needed a warm place to hide them, but where? He looked around searching for somewhere suitable, somewhere where they wouldn't be discovered.

The ledge above the cooker hood - that was it! He reached up and slid the plates to the back. He stepped back. Perfect, they were out of sight.

A door banged. Roberts froze. Someone was moving about. He rammed the incriminating evidence into the box and stuffed it into the sink cupboard.

"You're up late Mr. Roberts!" A guard was in the doorway. "What are you doing in here?"

"I couldn't sleep. What time is it?"

"It's after three, Sir."

Roberts filled a glass with water and drank. "I needed that."

The guard waited in the hallway until Roberts climbed the stairs and close his bedroom door.

Charlie Benson was up early, eager to confront Roberts, to get his money. He arrived for work, filled a kettle and went to the sink cupboard. The box was still there but it had been opened. There was a shrill whistle; the kettle. Filling the teapot Charlie spilled boiling water on the worktop. It ran down the cupboard door unto the floor. Charlie composed himself, prepared a breakfast tray and took it upstairs. Nervously, he knocked on the bedroom door.

Max Roberts was by the window, reading a book.

Charlie put the tray down. Stood with his back obscuring the camera and pointed to a slip of paper on the tray. "I want paying,"

Roberts poured himself a cup of tea and swallowed a mouthful. "Do you know what I'm going to do when I get out of here? I'm going to pay my debts and celebrate being free. Does that sound reasonable to you?"

Then Charlie understood - Roberts was a prisoner. He had no money. "Later," he'd said but would he pay later, would he pay at all?

Angry with himself, for being stupid, for trusting Roberts, for getting involved Charlie went back to the kitchen. He needed leverage, something to negotiate with. The box - that was it.

Max Roberts looked drunk when he went to bed just before midnight. The control room monitor showed him staggering up the stairs carrying a bottle of scotch. At two o'clock he got up and looked through the bedroom window. A red glow illuminated a face at the end of the drive. A sentry was smoking by the gates. Satisfied the house was quiet Roberts swallowed a slug of whisky and crept down to the kitchen taking the bottle of scotch with him.

He unpacked the CRISPR box and lifted the culture plates down from the ledge where he'd hidden them. He held the first plate up to the light. "Damn." Nothing. The E-Coli hadn't taken. The second plate was the same. The culture was dead - useless. Only one left. His hand shook as he raised the last plate and peered at it. "Thank God!" They were there, just as the instructions predicted, white spots; the bacteria had worked. He poured another drink and swallowed it. It was time to use the centrifuge; to make the dose for an injection. There could be no mistakes - the risks were huge but he was committed now. There was no going back.

The centrifuge! It wasn't in the box. Roberts searched the kitchen. A saucepan slid from a cupboard and hit the floor. Roberts froze, listening for voices - for guards' footsteps. Nothing. He went into the pantry, scanning the shelves. He'd settle with Charlie Benson later. Where was it? He had to find the centrifuge. Think! Think! Where would it be? Then he found it, hidden behind the vegetable rack. Roberts carried the centrifuge back to the kitchen and sat down. There was work to do and he didn't have much time.

The whisky bottle was empty buy the time he'd finished preparing the dose. Roberts pointed the syringe up and squeezed, expelling a drop of liquid. He swallowed, tightened the tourniquet on his arm, selected a blood vessel and pressed home the needle. He shuddered. The needle slipped and came out. A drop of blood ran down his arm. Roberts' teeth ground together biting, vice like, on nothing. He concentrated and tried again, further up the arm. The needle pierced the skin and disappeared. He shut his eyes and slowly emptied the syringe into his vein. Roberts fumbled, dropping the syringe. He tried to focus. The syringe was standing, dart like, its point embedded in the wooden floor.

CHAPTER 27

Sandra Tate touched the dressing on her arm. It was tender but she didn't care. It felt good knowing the microchip was out, that she was no longer living with lethal poison in her body. She sat on the upturned dinghy and looked out to sea. A man was using a stick ball pitching the ball into the sea for a spaniel to swim after.

"Are you pleased to be back at work?" she asked.

Simon didn't answer.

The dog waded ashore with the ball, shook itself and ran off.

"Sally.... SALLY," shouted the man. The dog sat, toying with the ball, ignoring him.

Simon drew a circle in the sand with his toe. "Yes. I was surprised when they asked me to go back to Harland Digital. The Prime Minister is keeping Regis, says the DNA database is a valuable tool."

They got up and walked along the beach.

"Why didn't Hughes destroy the coat after the fire?"

"I guess he needed a hold over Roberts," said Simon. "Maybe he kept it as a sort of insurance. Perhaps blackmail him. Tell me again about Petch. What happened?"

"The day Hughes was arrested, Petch was in the Ship Inn drunk. He shouted at the television screen when they said the Prime Minister had left the building. Alun went to calm him down. He swore at Alun and stormed out."

Simon's mobile phone rang.

"Simon, it's C.J. I hear you're back at Harland." C.J. Hunt's Texan drawl was unmistakable. "I have something for you, a peace offering."

"What do you mean, a peace offering?"

"I knew Lucas was cheating you but the deal he offered me was a peach. I couldn't turn it down. Geez, I'm sorry. Listen, before he died John Hume asked me to do something. He asked me to check a DNA profile, yours, and see if I could find a match."

"Why did he do that?"

"Hume said you had a twin sister you were looking for. Said he found a record saying she'd been adopted by folks in North Carolina."

Simon squeezed Sandra's hand and grinned. "You're saying my sister Pamela's alive?"

"No. I'm not saying that." CJ Hunt paused... "I didn't bother looking. Then, when I heard you were dead, there was no point in searching the database. What the hell for? I wasn't interested. Hell. There was other stuff going on."

The sun disappeared behind a cloud. A gust of wind blew dry sand across the beach stinging their faces. Simon turned away and held the phone close to his ear. "So what's the peace offering?"

"I'm offering to search our DNA database.... If you still want to know."

"Thanks C.J. Yes. That would be good."

"What did he say?" asked Sandra as they walked back to the village.

"He's going to search for my sister, Pamela. Thinks she's in America. Come on. I'll buy you a drink."

The Ship Inn was crowded. They joined Gary Bridger

at the bar and ordered.

"Don't look," said Sandra. "Petch is over there playing the fruit machine."

"Let's go outside," said Simon.

They cleared empty glasses from a table in the beer garden and sat down.

"Have you heard?" asked Gary. "Roberts is in hospital. He's critical. They said on the news it was a drugs overdose."

"No! When?" asked Sandra.

Petch appeared in the doorway, ambled over and sat down.

"This morning," said Gary.

"Simon, 'is good to see 'ya."

"And you Petch. You look like you've been having a good time."

Petch grinned.

Simon raised his glass. "Here's to the death of a murderer and a tyrant. May he rot in Hell."

"Dead, 'ho's dead?" asked Petch.

"He isn't dead yet but we're drinking to the death of Max Roberts," said Simon.

Petch scratched his chin. "Not dead! He killed Monk... Monk, my best mate. He should be dead."

Max Roberts didn't die, he recovered and was returned to house arrest. It was a bright autumn morning when the Attorney General Sir Jason Langwade came to see Roberts for a second time. He was shown into the lounge.

Roberts was reading a book. He didn't get up. "Gibbon was wrong. Commodus was weak, not wicked. His simplicity and timidity rendered him the slave of his attendants, who gradually corrupted his mind. His cruelty was the ruling passion of his soul."

"You're reading The Decline and Fall of the Roman Empire," said the Langwade.

"It passes the hours," said Roberts. "Leaders have to be

strong. Do you know his enemies tried to poison him? He vomited up the poison. They failed so he was drowned in a bath. An appropriate end for a weak man."

Roberts waved Langwade to a seat.

"The Crown Prosecution Service have examined the evidence relating to the fire at Coed Mawr," said Langwade. "We all agree, you have no case to answer. Arrangements are being made for your release."

Roberts placed his book on the table. "Good."

"You don't seem surprised."

"I'm not. You said arrangements. What arrangements?"

"These are our terms. The media will be told you have recovered from a serious illness and are retiring from public life. You will resign as leader of the NPP. I have a draft of your resignation letter with me. Your ministerial pension will be enhanced and a suitable grace and favour home provided."

"What about security?"

"Personal protection officers are provided for all retired Prime Ministers Mr. Roberts."

"I want a suitable car and a chauffeur."

"Naturally," said Sir Jason.

"I had nothing to do with the way Hughes ran the OIS. He was a maverick. You will publish a report exonerating me from any blame. I want my reputation restored. Do you understand; there's to be clear water between my role as Prime Minister, trying to protect the people, and the thugs in the OIS."

"Hughes is being dealt with by the courts. He will go to prison for a very long time but I don't..." Langwade frowned, reconsidering what he was about to say. "I think we can find a form of words." He waited for the next demand.

But there were no more demands. Roberts had what he wanted; his freedom, a promise to restore his reputation and a pension for life.

CHAPTER 28

Vincent Kidger threw the report down. It skidded across his desk and onto the floor. The Chief Constable of Dyfed Powys was furious. He pressed the intercom. "Get me the Attorney General's office. I want to speak to Sir Jason Langwade." He picked up the report and waited for the call to come through.

The phone rang. "Sir Jason isn't available," said his secretary. "I have his deputy Sir Henry Fellows, the Solicitor General on the line."

"Put him through," said Kidger. "Sir Henry, I've just read the Crown Prosecution Service's report on the fire at Coed Mawr. It's a travesty. The DNA evidence was plain enough. Roberts was at the fire. We know Hughes was involved. Now Roberts has turned on him, he'll talk. You can't let Roberts get away with it. We all know he murdered Mr. and Mrs Jackson."

"You're probably right Vincent but a decision has been made at the highest level. We will not be prosecuting Roberts. The case would be thrown out. I'm sorry."

"What do I tell Simon Reece? That we know who killed his parents but we aren't going to do anything about it?"

"Tell him the truth," said Sir Henry. "He's not a fool.

He'll understand."

Simon was in Cambridge when Kidger phoned him. The Chief Constable said he had news about Simon's parents. He refused to discuss the details on the phone. Simon drove to Wales the following day. Gary Bridger met him at Police Headquarters and went with him to see the Chief Constable.

They were taken to a conference room on the second floor. Coffee and tea had been placed ready on a tray. A picture window filled the room with light.

"Has he said anything to you?" asked Simon as they waited.

Gary shook his head. "Only that he wanted to talk to both of us. We're honoured."

"What do you mean?" asked Simon.

"Chocolate biscuits." Gary pointed to the tray.

Kidger arrived. "Sorry for keeping you waiting. A meeting. "Tea, coffee?"

"No thanks," said Simon.

"Thank you for coming Mr. Reece. Gary, I wanted you here because you're involved and I know your father attended the fire at Coed Mawr. Please take a seat. I'll get straight to the point. The Crown Prosecution will not be charging Max Roberts with the murders of William and Florence Jackson."

"Why not? My parents died in the fire," said Simon. "You have the evidence; the coat, his DNA was on it. He's the murderer."

"I believe he is and should be brought before a court but the thing is - it isn't."

"What isn't? You're not making any sense."

"The DNA on the coat matches Roberts' DNA, on the database," said Kidger, "but it isn't Roberts' DNA."

"Now I'm confused," said Gary Bridger. "If it matches the record on the database it has to be Roberts' DNA."

Kidger picked up a folder and handed it to Simon.

"Read this, then you'll understand."

25th June Max Robert admitted to Papworth Hospital with suspected blood poisoning, cause initially unknown. Contents of a syringe removed from the safe house indicates Roberts injected himself with a Cas-9 CRISPR genome editing agent....

"Genome editing? What does that mean?" asked Simon.

"It means he attempted to alter his DNA profile," said Kidger, "and that's the problem. They say he nearly died..." The police chief closed the folder. "Even though the CPS are confident he's the arsonist, the evidence on the coat is compromised. It's the only evidence they have to offer and it won't stand up to scrutiny. The whole case would be hanging by a single thread. The CPS prosecutes and his defence barrister simply says, 'Your database must be wrong. Where's your proof it was my client?' - Do you see? Roberts would walk from the court a free man."

"What about Hughes? He was there. His evidence would finger Roberts."

Kidger shrugged. "I asked the same question and was told Hughes is a murderer, a proven liar and an unreliable witness with an axe to grind. He hates Roberts. Roberts hung him out to dry. Anything he says will be disregarded. I don't like this any more than you but there's nothing we can do. It's a political decision made at the top."

"Doesn't his attempt to change his DNA prove his guilt?"

"You're telling me that's it? He kills my mother and father - and NOTHING is going to be done about it?" Simon stood up. "He didn't just kill my parents. Roberts destroyed hundreds of lives. He's a monster. Why are you protecting him?"

"I'm not protecting him. You weren't listening to me." Kidger took back the folder and closed it. "I said I don't like it but there's nothing I can do."

Simon drove to Coed Mawr. He wanted to talk to Sandra, to tell her about the meeting with Kidger, to ask her advice. It was one o'clock. He turned the car radio on.

"... the enquiry clears Downing Street of any involvement. Prime Minister Roberts' advisers, it says, did not make him aware of the OIS snatch squads or how the detention camps were run. However, he accepts the vile crimes perpetrated by Director Hughes and the OIS happened on his watch. This morning he resigned as leader of the National People's Party. The report is already being called a cover up by opposition groups who are calling for Roberts to be investigated by the International Criminal Court for crimes against humanity. One thing is certain - this story isn't over yet..."

Simon's phone rang. "Simon, it's C.J. I found her, your sister Pamela. She's living in Raleigh, North Carolina. She wants to meet you."

"She's alive..." Simon swallowed as his emotional dam burst. He remembered his parents' funeral, the battered suitcase, the cages at Lingham, undressing the guards' corpses, watching the young Asian boy, Awan Jarwar, die in agony.

"Simon... Are you there? Did you hear what I said? Pamela, she's alive. She's Doctor Madison Clark now. Has two kids."

"Yes... I'm here." Simon pulled over and rested his forehead on the steering wheel.

"Simon."

"...That's great C.J. Thanks."

Sandra was in the garden when Simon arrived. "Have you heard the news? They say Roberts isn't responsible for what the OIS did. What's the matter? You look awful." She followed him into the house.

"Kidger told me the gutless bastards at the CPS won't prosecute him for killing my parents." A tear ran down Simon's cheek. He fell into her arms.

"Shhhh," said Sandra and held him.

"My sister's alive."

"What?"

"She's a doctor with two children. I'm an uncle." He wiped his eyes. "Imagine that."

The following morning Simon went to The Fisherman's Yarn looking for Petch. It was early, before eleven o'clock, but the bar was crowded with drinkers spending their dole money. Simon pushed his way to the bar. The landlady, a big woman with a broken nose watched him, gimlet eyed.

"A whisky," said Simon. "Make it a large one. I'm looking for someone."

"Who might that be?" She drained the optic and placed the glass on the bar. "That's six pounds eighty."

"A friend of mine." Simon handed her a ten pound note. "Keep the change. His name's Petch. Has parachute regiment wings tattooed on his right arm."

"You're not a copper." The landlady's eyes glanced momentarily to a door with the word 'lounge' on in. "What you want him for?"

Simon picked up the glass. "Cheers," he said and moved towards the door.

"You can't go in there." She stepped from behind the bar blocking the way. "It's private."

Simon pushed her aside.

Petch was, alone in the lounge, nursing a glass of beer. No lights were on. The room was cold, uninviting. It smelt of greasy leftovers and stale alcohol. Soiled upholstery lined the yellowing walls.

"Here." Simon placed his glass in front of Petch.

The landlady was in the doorway. "I told you. This room's private."

"You said Petch wasn't here." Simon held up a fifty pound note. "To hire your private room."

The woman looked at Petch, hesitated and snatched the money.

"Shut the door," ordered Simon and sat down. "How are you Petch? You look like shit."

"You know how I am." Petch grinned proudly. "I'm pissed."

"I've a job for you. If you're interested." Their eyes met.

"A job... You'd employ me? I'm a soldier." Petch emptied his beer glass and placed it upside-down on the table. "Fuck... I was a soldier."

"So what are you now if you're not a soldier? What are you going to do Petch?"

"Fuck knows." He picked up the whisky glass. "Cheers. Get pissed."

Simon leaned forward. "I want to kill someone."

"You want me to kill someone." Petch drained the whisky. "Why didn't you say so. Alright. How much?"

"No. I've got to do it."

"You're mad." Petch chuckled. "FUCK OFF. GO ON. FUCK OFF."

Simon turned scarlet. "Is that it?" He stood up.

"Not so cocky now are you Mr. Computer Man?" sneered Petch. "You come here, bold as fucking brass, telling me you want to kill someone. Who is it? Who do your hate so much?"

"Roberts," said Simon quietly. "Max Roberts."

Petch stopped smiling. "That would be something."

Simon sat down again. "So you'll help me."

"How d'you want to kill him Simon?" Petch moved closer. "A knife? Strangle him? Poison? Do you want him to die slowly? To watch the horror on his face - see the pain - to enjoy the spectacle?"

"No." Simon wiped perspiration and globules of spit from his face... "I don't know."

"You don't know?.. MAUREEN," yelled Petch.

The woman appeared at the door.

"Bring us two whiskies, large ones... You can't rush this Simon. Do you care if you're caught?"

"I don't understand."

"Are you willing to go to prison?"

Getting caught, prison - The word formed a knot in Simon's stomach.

The landlady returned with the drinks.

"You've gone white," said Petch and pushed a glass across the table. "You afraid Simon?" He grinned. "Drink it." He lifted the glass to Simon's lips. "Numbs the pain."

Simon sipped, swilling the whisky around his mouth. He swallowed and felt the warmth relieve the pain in his gut.

"Will you help me?"

"Twenty thousand pounds," said Petch quietly. "In cash, in advance."

"I'll pay you half tomorrow and the rest when it's done, when Roberts is dead."

Simon returned to Carmarthen the following morning.

Petch, shaved and looking presentable, was waiting at the side of the road. He threw a bag in the back and got into the car. "You got the money?"

"It's on the back seat," said Simon as they pulled away. Petch reached over and picked up a hessian bag, spilling bundles of notes as he yanked it into the front of the car."

"Ten thousand pounds, as we agreed. Are you going to count it?"

"Do I need to?..." Petch pushed the bag into the foot-well. "I trust you."

"This is Shawcross Manor where Roberts lives." Simon handed Petch a photograph. "It's near Peterborough."

"Nice," said Petch.

They drove to Peterborough and booked rooms in a tavern.

The landlord stood behind the bar and watched Simon sign the register."Mr. Parson and Mr. Walsh. How long are you gents staying?"

"Two maybe three nights," replied Simon and glanced

at Petch.

The landlord passed them two keys. "We're not busy so that's fine. Do you want to pay for two nights?"

Simon paid cash for the rooms. "I'm ready for a drink." He studied the beer pumps. "I've never heard of Green Devil. What's it like?"

The landlord pulled a taster into a spirit glass and gave it to Simon. "It's a local craft beer. Quite strong."

"It's good. I'll have a pint," said Simon. "You should try it, Tony."

"No thanks," said Petch. "Give me an orange squash. No ice."

"Squash?" asked Simon. "Don't you want a beer?"

"I said no alcohol. Buy me a beer when we're done."

They were the only customers eating in the tavern that night. After they'd eaten, Simon opened his laptop.

"Go to Google Earth," said Petch. "You said he lives at Shawcross Manor. Let's have a look." They magnified the image and studied the layout.

"There might be a good place." Petch pointed to a hedge lined field, at the bottom of the screen. "Plenty of cover." He held a table knife against the scale and used it to estimate the distance to the house. "Looks like six hundred metres. We need to find out if there's a line of sight. Did you load the Ordnance Survey map like I told you?"

Simon nodded and clicked a Garmin icon on the desktop. A map appeared on the screen.

Petch used the cursor to draw a straight line between the hedge and the house. He read the numbers on the plot. "I was right. Six hundred and forty metres and the house is twenty one metres lower than the field. We'll be hidden and able to retreat without being seen. There are no footpaths so we shouldn't be disturbed. We'll have a look tomorrow."

Simon was going to order another drink when Petch stopped him.

"Why?" asked Simon.

"We need clear heads tomorrow."

Petch had changed. He was focused, thinking ahead and the swagger was gone.

"Is Petch your surname?" asked Simon. "I've often wondered."

"No, it's Church."

"Church! So where did Petch come from? It can't be your first name."

Petch shrugged. "My first name's Peter, Peter Church - Petch - get it? It was my nickname in the army."

Simon tried to imagine him as Peter. The name didn't fit.

The following morning was overcast and threatened rain. They dressed in dark walking clothes, drove to Shawcross, parked a mile from the village and hiked across the fields to the hedge Petch had chosen on the map. They didn't speak and were careful not to be seen as they approached. Petch unpacked binoculars and a groundsheet from his rucksack, spread it out and the two men lay on the ground. Shawcross Manor, gothic, large and rambling was in the valley below them.

"Now we wait and watch," said Petch. He scanned the house with the binoculars and handed them to Simon. "You have the first shift."

Simon adjusted the focus and looked at the manor house. They had a perfect view. He could even see the furniture in the rooms. A policeman, cradling a weapon, was standing by wrought iron gates leading to a lane. A man was, raking the lawn, at the back of the house.

It was after four and Petch was watching, when the gardener left. A short while later the police sentry was relieved. At half past a black Mercedes approached along the lane. The gates opened. The vehicle drove to the front of the house and stopped. Two men got out of the car. One opened the rear door.

"He's there, Roberts, getting out of the car," said Petch quietly. They watched Roberts go into the house. A light went on. He reappeared in an upstairs window.

"That must be his bedroom," said Simon.

The curtains closed.

It was dark when they got back to the tavern.

"How many times have you fired a rifle?" Petch asked during dinner.

"I was in the Air Cadets. Did some shooting then."

"You're telling me you haven't fired a rifle for more than twenty years? Fuck." Petch frowned. "What weapon?"

"A .22 Martini Action. We used to shoot on a twenty-five yard range in the basement of the drill hall."

"And you think that's the same as hitting a man at six hundred metres?"

Simon put his knife and fork down. "You don't think I can do it, do you?"

"You'll miss. Then what?.." Petch was staring at Simon. "You won't get a second shot..."

Simon didn't answer.

"Are you having second thoughts?"

"Yes... No. I mean... No. I'm not having second thoughts."

"We've got to be sure. If this is going to work, I need to see you shoot. I'll think of something."

Simon and Petch observed Shawcross Manor for three days then, believing they knew enough about Roberts' routine and his security, they returned to Carmarthen.

Petch got out of the car and grabbed his bag. "I'll ring you when I have the rifle." He turned and walked away.

CHAPTER 29

Sandra was out when Simon arrived at Coed Mawr. He let himself into the house and was asleep in a chair when she returned.

"The wanderer returns."

Simon opened his eyes. "Sorry I dropped off."

She stood over him. "No phone calls. No, I'm fine. How are you Sandra?.. Where've you been?"

He sat up. "I'm Sorry I should have called. I've been working."

"WORKING, You're not working. I rang Harland and asked for you. They said you were taking a few days off. You've been with Petch. Haven't you?.. I know what you're doing. It's written all over your face." She stormed from the room.

Simon followed her to the kitchen. "Don't you understand? I have to do this."

Sandra was filling the kettle. "So you're going to kill a man because you think forty years ago he burned down a house killing your parents, two people you can't even remember." She slammed the kettle down and plugged it in."Admit it you don't even know what they looked like."

He moved towards her and reached out.

"Don't." She pushed him away. "...I think you'd better go."

Sandra held back the tears until the front door slammed.

It was late when Simon came back. He stumbled up the stairs, undressed dropping his clothes on the floor and slipped into bed."

"What time is it?"

"Half past eleven," said Simon. "I thought you were asleep."

"I've been lying here thinking." She turned over and snuggled up to him. "I'm frightened. Something terrible is going to happen."

"Shhhh. Nothing's going to happen to us. I promise." He held her.

"How can you say that? How can you be sure?"

Simon didn't answer. He was asleep.

Petch phoned the following day and told Simon to meet him at an old barn. "It's remote," he explained. "No one will be about."

The barn was in a small wooded valley. Simon walked down a narrow, muddy track to the barn. A section of corrugated roof had collapsed and hung at a perilous angle. It moved, with every puff of wind, clanking against the side of the barn.

Petch was sitting on the seat of a rusting, long abandoned, tractor. He pointed to a gun bag on the ground.

Simon unzipped the bag and took out the weapon. He examined the telescopic sight holding the gun up to look through it.

"Stop waving it about. It could be loaded," snapped Petch.

Simon pointed the gun at the floor. "It's a pellet gun."

"That's right. A .22 air rifle."

"Are you serious? I'm going to use an air gun."

Petch climbed off the tractor and took the gun from Simon. "No. I'm going to see you shoot with it." He pointed to the end of the barn. "See those little white targets on the corrugated wall. They're twenty-five metres away. I want to see you shoot. He gave the gun back to Simon and handed him a tin of pellets. "Go on. Load it. Let's see if you can hit one."

Simon broke open the barrel and fumbled, dropping a pellet. He took another, pushed it into the breech, aimed and fired. The pellet hit the sheet metal with a ping.

"Missed," said Petch. "Try again." The next shot also went wide.

Simon turned around. "What am I doing wrong?"

"Why are you pointing a weapon at me? Take your finger away from the trigger, put the safety on and point the gun at the ground. NOW," ordered Petch.

"Rule one. Assume at all times your gun is loaded and ready to fire. Never, never point it at someone unless you intend to use it..." Petch walked to the target. "You missed the target by a hundred millimetres. At six hundred and fifty metres you would be more than a metre wide. You've missed by nearly five feet." He shook his head. "Everything's wrong. Your breathing's wrong. The gun's going up and down like a see-saw. You're gripping it like a vice, trying to force your aim, and you have no balance. You're standing like John Wayne and snatching at the trigger like a cowboy."

His stupidity, pointing the gun at Petch and the dressing down un-nerved Simon. "I'm sorry... Will you show me?"

"Give me the gun." Petch took the weapon from Simon. "Let's start with your position. You won't be standing. The shot will be from a prone position." He laid down and demonstrated. "Your body needs to be at fifteen degrees from the line to the target. Like this. Here, you try."

Simon took the gun and laid down.

"It needs to feel natural, as if the gun wants to point at the target. When you shut your eyes and open them again it should still be pointing in the same place. When you breathe the gun will rise and fall. Breathe steadily and squeeze the trigger slowly as you exhale and the cross hairs are on the target. Don't jerk or you will miss. Try it."

Simon reloaded and fired.

"That's better. You hit an outer ring. Again."

The lesson continued until Petch was satisfied. "Five in the bull. A good grouping. I'll make a marksman out of you yet."

Petch and Simon met the following week in a wood. Simon followed Petch through the forest, up a steep bank, to a clearing overlooking the trees.

Petch took the gun bag from his shoulder and opened it. "It's a superb weapon, A Bergara hunting rifle. You couldn't ask for anything better and these," he produced a handful of bullets from a pocket, "are Creedmoor shells. They're boringly accurate, capable of MoA accuracy."

"MoA, what does that mean?"

"It means 'Minute of Accuracy'. They'll hit a one inch target at one hundred metres." Petch was enjoying himself. "All we need now is a marksman who knows how to use them. To make it simple for you, I've set the scope for the distance you will be firing from. Just centre the sight on the target and shoot. Down there, can you see it." He pointed at a white square on a tree. "That's Roberts. The range and elevation are right. Take your time and do exactly the same as you did with the air rifle. Remember, keep your aim steady after you squeeze the trigger and Simon, this gun has a recoil. Your shoulder will feel it."

Simon loaded the gun, took careful aim, waited until he was gently breathing out and pulled the trigger. The rifle discharged with a loud crack. The noise was louder than he expected. Simon felt the kick, the energy of the weapon. Its intoxicating authority. Here was power, the power of life or death. Simon grinned.

"A hit left side," said Petch and lowered his binoculars. "Feels good doesn't it? Try again."

Simon fired more shots. Petch adjusted the telescopic sight, correcting the aim. Simon fired again and again, enjoying the thrill of each hit.

They walked down to examine the target.

Petch grinned. "Well done. That's a difficult shot. You're ready. Look at this." He examined the back of the tree. "See the splinters. The bullets have ripped right through. Hit Roberts anywhere in the chest and the fucking job's done. He won't get up."

"Where did you get the rifle?" asked Simon. "It's a beautiful weapon."

"From a farmer. He boasted about going deer stalking with it. Loads of pictures on Facebook. Idiot even posted a picture of the gun safe he kept it in." Petch ripped the cardboard target from the trunk of the tree.

"You stole it?"

"Course I fucking stole it. What did you think? I'd ask to borrow it." Petch slung the gun over his shoulder. "The light's going. Let's get back."

Simon slept badly that night. His mind was in turmoil, replaying, their trip to Shawcross, the afternoon with Petch and the power of the rifle.

"Wake up." Sandra shouted. "You're having a nightmare."

Simon sat upright and wiped sweat from his eyes. The room was dark. Sandra was standing beside the bed.

"What were you dreaming about?"

"I don't know." Simon went to the bathroom. "I can't explain. I tried to warn you."

"You kept yelling, 'Get away, hide'. You nearly pushed me out of bed."

Simon splashed cold water on his face. "I'm sorry. I was trying to warn you. To save you."

"To save me from what?"

"I don't know," replied Simon.

But he did know. In his dream Simon was looking through a telescopic sight. He could see a house clearly and beyond it the sea. It made no sense. It was the wrong house. His aim moved back to the house. He resisted but his arms wouldn't obey.

Petch was talking. "The gun wants to point at the target."

A woman, was moving in one of the rooms. He watched, helpless, as he slipped the safety catch off and put his finger on the trigger. He shouted, to warn her, "GET DOWN, HIDE," but she didn't hear. She walked to the window and looked straight at him.

Simon returned to the bedroom. "He's not worth it."

"What do you mean? Who's not worth it?"

"Roberts. I don't have to kill him." He got back into bed.

"Come here," said Sandra and moved closer. "You never had to kill him. He's nothing to us."

Simon telephoned Petch the next morning. "You were right. I'm not a killer. I won't do it."

"Fuck," said Petch. "You telling me I stole the gun for nothing. Teaching you to shoot, all the time we spent lying in the mud watching his house, for nothing."

"I should never have asked you. It was stupid. I'm sorry."

"What about the money, the ten thousand pounds?"

"Keep it."

"Fucking right I'm keeping it," shouted Petch and hung up.

A camouflage clad figure crept slowly around a wheat field and lay in the mud behind a hedge. The ripe ears of wheat swayed in the breeze, bright and yellow. The man looked back to check his retreat wasn't visible. His face was hidden by a hood and mask. He unfastened a gun bag, slipped it off his shoulder and took out a sniper's rifle. He looked up at the brilliant blue sky, the branches overhead and the translucent green leaves shimmering in the sunlight.

Somewhere to his left a wood pigeon 'cooed' in the trees. He gently eased the barrel through the hedge and scanned Shawcross Manor through the telescopic sight. The house was quiet, a silent stage waiting for the final act.

An engine noise distracted the sniper; farm machinery. A combine harvester working the next field was coming closer. He hadn't planned for that. Would the driver, high in his cab, see him? The engine noise grew louder then faded as the machine turned. An hour passed. The combine stopped. A tranquil quiet settled across the countryside, deceptive, unreal. The assassin ate a chocolate bar, folded the wrapper neatly and stuffed it into his pocket. The sun was close to the horizon now. Roberts was late. Soon the light would fade.

A black Mercedes pulled up.

The sniper got into position, aimed at the limousine and slipped the safety catch off.

The driver got out and opened the rear door.

"Move," muttered the gunman.

Roberts stepped from the car.

There was a crack. Robert's fell to the ground with a small puncture mark in his back and a saucer sized hole in his chest.

The gunman crept away, leaving the rifle on the ground.

Leaning forward, Madison could see the Shard rising through the haze. Its pointed spire gleaming in the sunshine. "Look Scott, down there, London. We'll be landing soon."

The aircraft turned. It was lower now. Scott and his sister, Charlotte, had a better view of the ground, of the River Thames snaking through the city.

"There's the Tower of London," shrieked Scott.

"Le'me see," yelled his sister straining to see. "Mom, he won't let me see."

The plane levelled out.

"Will Uncle Simon be there to meet us?" asked Scott.

"Sure," said his mother. "He promised he'd be at the airport and, guess what? He told me we're 'gona ride on a boat pushed along by a pole."

The children pulled faces. Charlotte giggled.

"No he didn't," said Scott. "You made that up."

The overnight flight from North Carolina was the first to arrive at Heathrow. Madison and the children cleared immigration quickly. She shepherded Scott and Charlotte through baggage collection and customs into the terminal.

The doors opened and there, to greet them, were Simon and Sandra.

Simon was introducing himself to the children when his mobile phone rang. "Hello, who is this?"

"It's done," said Petch. "Remember our deal. You owe me the other ten thousand pounds."

ABOUT THE AUTHOR

Graham Watkins is a multi genre author who started writing when he retired. He cut his teeth researching and reinventing Welsh legends and myths, a four year project exploring Wales and its rich legacy of stories. Graham lives in a rambling farmhouse in the Brecon Beacons with his wife, a lunatic rescue dog called Sally and a motley collection of animals which at different times have included, chickens, ducks, geese, sheep and Welsh Black cattle. His neighbours describe him, not unkindly, as a hobby farmer who tries to write and gives talks about his writing to anyone who will listen.

You can learn more about his writing at https://www.grahamwatkins.info

OTHER BOOKS BY
GRAHAM WATKINS

Most titles are available as eBooks, in paperback and as
audio books.

Fiction

The Iron Masters
A White Man's War
The Sicilian Defence
Supernatural Stories
Welsh Legends and Myths
The Turnings of the Years - A collection of short
stories from Llandovery Writer's Group of which Graham
is a member.

Non Fiction

The Welsh Folly Book
Walking With Welsh Legends (Five Volumes)

Business

Exit Strategy
Birth of a Salesman
How to Sell Ice to Eskimos.
The Art of the Book Fair

39427269R00132

Printed in Poland
by Amazon Fulfillment
Poland Sp. z o.o., Wrocław